The Gettysburg Vampire

Susan Blexrud

CRIMSON
ROMANCE
Avon, Massachusetts

This edition published by
Crimson Romance
an imprint of F+W Media, Inc.
10151 Carver Road, Suite 200
Blue Ash, Ohio 45242

www.crimsonromance.com

ISBN 10: 1-4405-6028-5
ISBN 13: 978-1-4405-6028-6
eISBN 10: 1-4405-6027-7
eISBN 13: 978-1-4405-6027-9

Dedication

"WAR AT ITS BEST IS TERRIBLE, AND THIS WAR OF OURS, IN ITS MAGNITUDE AND IN ITS DURATION, IS ONE OF THE MOST TERRIBLE."—PRESIDENT ABRAHAM LINCOLN

"THROUGH BLOOD AND TEARS, THIS WAR HAS DEFINED US AS A NATION."— UNION COLONEL MALCOLM MCCLELLAN

Acknowledgments

I gratefully acknowledge the books of Michael and Jeff Shaara, including *The Killer Angels, Gods and Generals,* and *The Last Full Measure.* They brought voices to historical characters and formed the backbone of my research.

And thanks from the bottom of my heart to my dedicated critique group—Jeanne Charters, Beth Robrecht, and Tara Horne.

Prologue

1863

The locomotive sped silently past Union Colonel Malcolm McClellan, whose blank stare belied his shock. No whistle pierced the air. No smoke billowed from the massive steam engine. No vibration shook the ground. A chill breeze had stirred the silence and set him gazing to the northeast through the mounting dusk. Otherwise, he would have missed the Stonewall Jackson altogether. Summer granted no chilling breezes. Malcolm looked down the line at his men, huddled behind the trees at their makeshift camp in northern Virginia.

"Did you see that, colonel?" Clayton asked, his voice as shaken as the air. "That sucker just busted on through. Didn't slow down a mite." The men had spent the previous night pulling up a large section of track. Any normal train would have ground to a halt or derailed.

"It didn't need to slow down, Clay," Malcolm said. "It seems to have levitated." Malcolm stared at the empty horizon where the train had sliced through at breakneck speed. His heart raced.

"Pardon me, colonel, but what does that mean?" Jack asked.

"I believe the train flew, gentlemen." Malcolm stooped and picked up a rock. He flung it in the direction the train had sped.

Jack collapsed to his knees. "Good Lord, colonel. I'd figure I was crazy if we hadn't all seen the same thing. We did all see the same thing?" He looked at his fellow soldiers, who all nodded. "You think that was the ghost train, colonel?"

Malcolm drew in a deep breath, and then blew it out with a cough. "I'm sure of it." He helped Jack to his feet. Rampant rumors of the ghost train had circulated for months, but actually seeing it had caught Malcolm unaware. His stomach churned.

"So, what do we do now, colonel?" Henry's voice squeaked. "Want William and me to mount up and follow the train?"

Malcolm removed his hat and wiped his brow with a handkerchief. "I don't believe you could catch it, not at the speed that train was traveling. Our orders from General Meade were to intercept the train, and since we can't derail it, I'd like to try to get on it. I think the only way to do that is to entice it to stop."

"What you think that train'll stop for, colonel? Dancing girls?" Jack chuckled nervously.

Malcolm narrowed his eyes. "No, Jack. I'm no expert on ghosts, but I imagine the only thing that can stop that train is death. If I had to guess, I'd say the Stonewall Jackson is some kind of latter-day death carriage collecting newly minted souls. And there are plenty of them these days on both sides of the conflict, though being a Confederate train, I doubt it would take kindly to our Yankee souls." Malcolm's men looked back at him with questioning stares.

"I hope you're not suggesting one of us volunteer to be a casualty, colonel." William glanced sideways at Malcolm.

"No, William, I'm suggesting we *pose* as casualties."

Again, all four men looked puzzled.

"This time tomorrow, we'll stage a scene right here where we tore up the tracks. We'll make it look like we were ambushed trying to fix the ties. Just William and me. We can smear some rabbit blood on our clothes and lie by the tracks. The rest of you can stand watch from behind the trees."

"In your blue uniforms, they'll know you're Union, colonel," Henry said. "Only Rebs would be trying to fix Confederate tracks."

"We won't be in uniform, Henry. "

"Surely not just in your skivvies, colonel."

Malcolm smiled. "I'm afraid so." He patted the lieutenant's shoulder, and the churning in his stomach calmed as his plan coalesced.

"Then what, colonel?" William asked. "When they see we're not dead, what's to keep them from making it so?"

Malcolm squinted into the afternoon sun. "I don't know, William, but if they think we're Rebs, we shouldn't be in immediate danger." He half grinned. "You've been wounded before, haven't you, Lieutenant?"

"Yessir, at Antietam."

"So was I, at Gettysburg. I still have pain in my shoulder, and I've seen you favor your right leg. I believe we can seem wounded in a way that would fool the ghosts. From what little I know about them, ghosts aren't typically violent. They'll stop to pick up dead recruits, but I don't think they'd do us any harm once they see we're still alive."

"Colonel McClellan, sir, pardon me, but I think you're assuming a lot about the nature of ghosts, when you've never even met one."

"They were once people just like us, William. Follow my lead. I did Shakespeare at the Point." Malcolm smiled. "There's something about performing that frees a man."

"Pardon me, colonel, but I'm no actor. I'm not sure they'd believe me, sir." William removed his cap and twisted it in his hands. "I've never been a good liar, and I think they'd see right through me."

"Well, that should even the odds, William, since you'll be able to see right through them," Henry said. "You know, them being ghosts and all."

The men chuckled, and Malcolm nodded. "All right, then, William. If you feel you'd be a liability, join the other men. You can all be my audience."

"You sure you want to do this, colonel?" Henry asked. "I don't know how much help we can be. I mean, you can't shoot a ghost, right? They're already dead."

Malcolm looked to the northeast, where, he assumed, this time tomorrow, the train would again materialize. "If you've got a better idea, by all means speak up. But we don't have much time."

Malcolm turned from the tracks and headed back to their camp. He quickened his pace as the adrenalin pumped through his system and his plan took shape. He'd feign a head injury. That would make the most sense. He'd appear to be knocked out, and then he'd "regain consciousness" once he was aboard the train.

He thought back to his acting days at West Point. In his role as Shylock, he'd mastered the character of a miserly old moneylender. Surely he could play a wounded Confederate soldier. And if he said he was from Maryland, he wouldn't have to affect a Southern accent, though he might need to practice a rebel yell.

Though he'd been skeptical of the ghost train's existence, he couldn't deny what he and his men had just seen. Over the past year, the legend of the Stonewall Jackson had become fodder for local storytellers, and the tales swirling about the inhabitants of the train had escalated from ghosts to other more dreadful creatures like vampires. Malcolm had seen evidence of diaphanous spirits on the battlefield and felt the prickle of eerie presences. He could fathom the existence of ghosts. But vampires?

Chapter One

November

Kyle Matson leaned close to Abby Potter. "That vampire is about as scary as a hand puppet," he whispered in her ear, and then he jumped out of his director's chair. He dismissed the cowering student actors with a quick wave. "Take five. No, take ten. Oh, hell, let's just wrap for the day."

Abby bit her lip. She understood Kyle's reaction, even agreed with him a little, though she'd never tell her students that. She reached for the hand of the female lead, who reclined on a tufted chaise, waiting for a neck bite that never came.

The student picked up her parasol and slunk off the set. The male lead, playing a vampire, patted his exaggerated widow's peak, shrugged, and exited stage left. Abby hoped he hadn't paid too much for that haircut.

"That vampire is a joke," Kyle ranted after the students left.

Abby's frustration rose to the surface. She shook a finger at Kyle. "Don't criticize my students. I've said it before, and I'll say it again. I need to go to Philly and hang around the Goth clubs for a night or two. Bet I could find a decent would-be vampire."

"I need a convincing thespian, not just someone who *looks* like a vampire." Kyle slapped the script to his thigh. "Besides, we shouldn't use actors from outside the college." As head of the theater department, his word ruled.

Abby sighed. "The holiday production is always a pain. Students are more focused on finals and going home for Christmas than trying out for a play. Even the actors I depend on most have begged out of this one."

Kyle patted Abby's arm. Actually, a punch would be more accurate. "I know, and they'd usually jump through hoops for you." Kyle's smile didn't reach his eyes. "We've had luck with professors in the past. How about Malcolm McClellan?"

The mere mention of the man's name made Abby jerk with a shiver that radiated head to toe. "He's intense enough, that's for sure." *Also, broodingly sexy.*

"And according to coeds, handsome enough. Besides, he's a Civil War re-enactor."

"You call that acting? Just because he can wield a rifle and gallop across a battlefield doesn't mean he could play a bloodsucker."

"He obviously gets off on being macho." Kyle looked her directly in the eyes. "That's the kind of guy we're looking for."

Abby's hands went clammy. She didn't want to look like a wuss in front of Kyle, so she balled her fists and steeled her resolve. "Oh, all right. I'll go ask him. But if he says no, I'm on an all-out search for the scariest vampire I can find, which means going to a Goth club. It will kick the supporting cast performances up a notch if we have a good ghoul in the lead."

Abby scuffed out of the theater and blinked into the bright winter sky. She'd spent the morning painting sets, and though she'd rather not confront Dr. McClellan in jeans and an old sweater that had shrunk in the wash, she needed to get this over with.

Snowflakes stuck to her eyelashes, and she pulled her blazer tighter around her as she strode across campus. At that moment, Abby longed to head in a different direction, maybe to the campus coffee shop for a mocha latte. She loved her job as associate professor in the theater department. She lived for the thrill of helping young actors hone their craft, but she dreaded the yearly challenge of finding a decent cast for the holiday production. And this year she had an additional burden; she'd written the play.

As much as she didn't want to talk to Dr. McClellan, she had to admit Kyle was right. The professor would make an ideal vampire. He was certainly physical perfection. Tall, broad shouldered, and narrow hipped, there wasn't an ounce of anything but muscle on his imposing frame. His face was *GQ* chiseled, with a strong nose and full lips. But eye candy didn't begin to describe him. His larger-than-life demeanor could fill a room. She'd taken a Civil War history class from him in her sophomore year, and in spite of the fact that he'd scared the poop out of her, he'd also inspired her.

She recalled him striding around his classroom, weaving through the aisles of desks, painting word pictures of a battle. And then he would stop, planting his ice-blue eyes on a random student to inquire, "If you had been General Longstreet, would you have carried out Robert E. Lee's orders?" You didn't dare come to class unprepared. He put you there—in the midst of the conflict. You could almost smell the gun smoke and hear the cries of the men as he described the horrific realities of war like he'd been there. Because of his example, she'd decided to become a teacher. She'd also developed a serious crush on him.

Right before commencement, she'd gone to his office to let him know that he'd made a difference in her life. He'd listened to her, his expression grave, and then he nodded toward the door. Not a word, just a dismissive nod. Shaken, she'd slunk from his office, vowing not to cross his path again. How could the man be so passionate about history, yet so cold to his students? So much for her crush.

After graduation from Gettysburg and her subsequent master's from NYU, she accepted a position in the theater department at her alma mater. She'd seen the professor on rare occasions at faculty functions, where they'd briefly locked eyes, but he kept to himself most of the time. Now, as she traversed the quad to the history building, her feet dragged as though chained to cannon balls. She hoped she'd be able to make her request without breaking out in a cold sweat.

Rather than ride the elevator to the third floor, she forced herself up the stairs, practicing what she planned to say with each step. Opening the door from the stairwell, she looked down the hall, lined with the offices of tenured professors. Taking off her blazer and draping it over her arm, she sucked in a deep breath and reminded herself that Dr. McClellan was just a man. He put his pants on one leg at a time. *Scratch that.* The image of him getting dressed gave her heart a jolt that was not conducive to calming her nerves.

She rapped gently on the door that read "Malcolm H. McClellan, Ph.D."

Hearing what sounded like an agitated "*Entrez,*" she eased the door open. The professor did not look up from his desk. "Essays are due Friday. No excuses."

He wore a black turtleneck, sleeves pushed up to the elbows revealing muscled forearms. His artistic hands rested on a stack of papers.

"I'm not a student, Dr. McClellan. I'm a professor. Perhaps you remember me?" Abby folded her arms, but then dropped them and settled for clasping her hands in front of her—less confrontational.

"So I see. Yes, I remember you." His intense gaze scanned her head to toe. Did she detect a hint of appreciation? "Turn around."

"Excuse me?" Was she being dismissed before she had a chance to say anything?

He laughed. "I just want to see if the orange paint you're wearing is just on the front of your jeans or whether you're entertaining onlookers from every direction."

Abby looked down. The left leg of her jeans had a streak of paint from thigh to knee. Rather than turn around, though, she looked over her shoulder and arched her back to check the rear view. One hip pocket sported an orange handprint. *Lovely.* Then she realized her posture made her breasts jut forward at the professor, and she overcompensated by wrapping her arms across her chest. *I'm behaving like an idiot.* Without waiting for an invitation, which might not be forthcoming, she plunked into the wooden chair opposite his desk. "I've seen worse," she said.

"Worse what?" He arched one eyebrow.

Worse what, my patootie. "Worse paint damage," Abby said. *Good time to change the subject.* "I believe the last time I saw you, you were charging down Seminary Ridge."

Professor McClellan arched the other eyebrow. "That's *Cemetery* Ridge, Miss Potter. I'd expect better from someone who received an 'A' in my class." He half smiled. "Is it still *Miss* Potter?"

"I'm surprised you remember my grade, professor." *And my name.* "And yes, it's still *Miss*." Abby said "miss" a bit too loudly. A frisson of anxiety skittered up her spine; or was it excitement?

"Call me Malcolm. We're on equal footing now."

Hardly. "All right, uh, Malcolm." She nearly choked on his name. "Let's get down to business, shall we?" She cleared her throat. "I'm in charge of the annual holiday production, and this year we're doing a play called *Vampire Train.* I know the legend of the Stonewall Jackson has been written to death, pardon the pun, but I've always been fascinated by the notion that there were more than ghosts on that train. So, some may think the subject's a bit morose for the holidays, but my play includes a vampire."

Professor McClellan, who had seemed only mildly interested in her spiel, rose from his chair and rounded his desk. He perched on the corner, directly in front of Abby, his long legs spread straight out and crossed at the ankles. Planting his hands on either side of his hips, he leaned forward. His piercing eyes practically burned a hole in her forehead. "What do you know of vampires, Abby?"

Whoa, he called me Abby. "Enough to write a play?" She hadn't meant it to sound like a question. She'd read a lot about vampires in preparation for the play. She almost wished they were real. There was something mighty sexy about that neck-biting business.

"I think not." He straightened to his full John Wayne height, and his already baritone voice lowered an octave. "Why did you come to me?"

The way he'd said "Come to me" made Abby's knees tremble, and she found herself inching toward him. She took a deep breath, and blurted out her request. "I thought, or rather, the head of the theater department thought, though I had to agree, reluctantly, well, not entirely reluctantly, that you would possibly, no probably, oh hell, definitely, make a good vampire."

He rubbed his gorgeous cleft chin. "Interesting concept."

While he contemplated, she jumped in. "I'm hoping to use this play as the springboard for a couple of student set designers to get jobs in New York when they graduate. In this economy, theater jobs are hard to find." *Had she appealed to his sense of fairness?*

"I'm quite busy—"

She trudged on. "The better the cast is, the better the production will be. You'd be doing it for the students."

He shook his head. "I'm afraid—"

"Think of how inspiring it would be for them."

He upped the volume. "I don't want to set a precedent."

This was becoming a pissing match, and she could tell from his tone that he wasn't going to budge. "Oh, forget it. I can find someone at a Goth club in Philly. You know, a vampire wannabe."

"You shouldn't go to one of those places alone. Unsavory characters hang out there. You wouldn't want to be bitten by someone unscrupulous."

What did he mean by that? "I can handle myself."

"I'm sure you can." His expression didn't match his words. "When do you suppose you'll make this trip?"

"Do you want to go with me?" *No, I didn't say that.* "I'll probably head there tonight. But don't do me any favors."

"As you'll recall, Abby, there was a coed murdered here several years ago. I simply don't want the college to experience any untoward publicity."

"Oh, right. This is about the college." Abby's eyes wandered around the professor's office, and then returned to a rock on his desk, probably from Little Round Top. "I guess you've played a lot of Civil War heroes." *Maybe I can show him I remembered something from his class.* "My favorite was Colonel Chamberlain. What he did on Little Round Top with that slew of soldiers from Maine was amazing."

"Slew?" He huffed. "Is that somewhere between a brigade and a regiment, Abby? The next time you refer to Colonel Joshua Lawrence Chamberlain, you might remember it was the 20th Maine Volunteer Infantry Regiment."

So much for saving face. "I'll be going, now." She got up from her chair and smoothed her jeans down. "Thank you, Malcolm." She turned, and with as much bravado as she could muster, knowing an orange handprint decorated her butt, walked slowly out of his office. She stopped at the door and said over her shoulder, "You know, Christmas is coming. It would be nice if you cut the students some slack on the essay deadline. It is all about the students, isn't it, Malcolm?"

*

Malcolm leaned back in his chair. His heartbeat thrummed, which was odd. It typically beat so slowly that any doctor would have declared him dead. Of course, dead he was. Feeling the beat of his heart was disquieting, yet exciting. He stared at the door Abby had just closed and listened to her footsteps fade down the hall. Humans wouldn't have heard the soft pad of her boots on carpet, but he had no problem detecting each step. Her stomping helped. He pinched the bridge of his nose.

Had he remembered her? How could he forget?

She'd always sat in the front row of his class, glued to him with those soulful hazel eyes. Other coeds regarded him lustfully, but she hung on his words. She seemed genuinely interested in what he was trying to convey, not simply entranced by his veneer. He knew she was special, which is why he'd avoided her. The last thing he needed was human entanglement. Once she left the college after her graduation, he thought he was safe from her allure. He could still see her blowing those golden blonde bangs out of her eyes as she labored over a quiz. He'd repressed the image of her pert nose, peachy skin, and bouncy breasts. But damn if she didn't come back to Gettysburg to teach, and inadvertently, to haunt him.

And now he had no choice; he had to rescue her. He'd been unable to save Sarah those many years ago, when duty to country trumped family, but he could keep Abby out of harm's way. She'd probably go to that Goth club decked out like a fang-banger with no idea of the danger she was in. So, there'd be no compartmentalizing this time. He'd have to see her again. And then what? Act in her play? He could feel his resolve melting like the November snow. For the first time since Sarah died, he considered the prospect of companionship . . . and passion.

Chapter Two

Awakened by distant cannon fire, Sarah reached across the bed for Malcolm. He wasn't there. She sat up and found him standing at the window in full uniform, gazing off in the distance.

He must have sensed her stirring. He didn't turn around, but said, "John Reynolds was killed yesterday in a skirmish at Herbst's Woods. He'd just arrived to assist Buford."

Sarah rushed to her husband, almost tripping on her long nightgown, and wrapped her arms around him. She pressed her face into his broad back. "Oh, darling, I'm so sorry. He was a good man. And poor Kate! She must be devastated."

Malcolm ran his hand through his thick hair. "We graduated together at the Point. There wasn't a better soldier—or man."

"I must go to Kate. Perhaps she'd like to stay with us a while."

Malcolm turned from the window and pulled Sarah close. "My love, that won't be possible. I just received orders from General Meade. The Confederates are heading this way, and I'm to lead the Pennsylvania cavalry." He took a deep breath and audibly exhaled. "You'll need to go to your sister's house in town. By this afternoon, I expect General Lee will have set up camp here."

"Here? At our house?" Sarah disengaged from Malcolm's embrace and fingered the embroidered flowers on the nightgown her sister had made for her trousseau. She looked out the window, staring westward. "Are you sure?"

"I'd bet on it," he answered. "The Army of the Potomac is forming its defensive line southeast of town, waiting for Lee's attack. The Rebs will most likely tramp through our property today, spend the night here, and head through town tomorrow. I've instructed Sully to take the animals east to the old homestead.

I'm sure the Rebs will help themselves to our vegetables, but I'll be damned if I let them take the cattle and swine."

Sarah's knees buckled, and she slid to the floor. She clamped her arms around Malcolm's legs and sobbed. "I won't let you go."

He caressed her shoulders. "I forget how inexperienced you are with the life of a soldier." His hands lifted her delicate body, the body he worshipped. He raised her chin, forcing her to look into his eyes. "This is my duty, Sarah. "

She thumped his chest with her fists, but then went limp in his arms. "I wish you were just a farmer."

He laughed and stroked her cheek. "It's a bit late for that. Besides, most of the farmers in Pennsylvania are soldiers now. " He led her to the armoire and took out her gray riding dress, laying it on the bed. "Get dressed, my love, and see me off. Once I've reported to General Meade, I'll visit you this evening at your sister's."

"Will you be able to leave your men with the Rebs coming?"

"They won't attack at night, but by tomorrow, I'm afraid every building in town will become a hospital."

Sarah covered her face with her hands. "I can't believe they're so close."

"Let's hope they respect our property. I've heard the Rebs are kinder than our side in that regard." He gathered her in his arms. Rubbing her back until she settled, he then cupped her buttocks, lifted her, and kissed her soundly.

That evening as the sun set, Malcolm rapped on Caroline's door, just off Baltimore Street.

Sarah answered and pulled him quickly into the house, leaping into his arms and peppering his face with kisses. "Oh, Malcolm, I behaved like such a child today. Can you forgive me?"

He returned her kisses fervently, and said, "Sarah, I cannot be cross with you."

She led him through the house to the back porch, where a garden bloomed with roses, and a gentle breeze furled the Pennsylvania state flag. "I wrote you a letter today." She withdrew the stationery from her cuff and handed it to him.

He passed the letter beneath his nose to inhale the lavender scent, and then handed it back to her. "Read it to me."

They sat together on the porch swing, and she unfolded the paper. Her hands trembled as she smoothed it out. "Dearest," she began. "Forgive me for adding a burden to your duty." She looked up at him plaintively, and he nodded for her to continue. "As you remarked, I am inexperienced, but I married you knowing full well that you are a soldier. I had hoped that when you returned this last time it would be for good. I suppose it was foolish of me, and wishful thinking, but I never thought the war would go on this long. Please be patient with me, and know that I live for you and our love. Nothing is more important to me than knowing your mind is clear when you lead your men. Know that I am yours forever, and that if your life should end in the service of our nation, I will carry your name for the rest of my life. No one could ever replace you, my dearest, and our time together will sustain me, whatever the future brings." A tear trickled down her cheek, and she quickly wiped it away. "Your adoring wife, Sarah." She folded the note, returned it to its envelope, and fitted it into his breast pocket, just above his heart.

He patted his pocket. "I will keep it here." He rose from the swing and held a hand out to her. "I have to return to camp before dawn, but nothing would please this soldier more than to hold his beloved."

She stepped into his embrace, pressing her face against his chest. "My sister prepared the guest room for us. The bed's small for two, though."

Malcolm kissed the top of her head. "No matter. We will be one."

Chapter Three

Abby chose her outfit for the evening carefully. It wouldn't do to look like a virgin at a Goth club. She figured she could get away with a turtleneck, leggings, and knee-high stiletto boots, all in black. The boots added three inches to her five foot four frame. Like five foot seven was threatening. Oh, well, she'd make it up in attitude.

Borrowing as much chain jewelry as she could find, she sprayed a few purple streaks in her blonde bangs, hung spider web earrings from her ears, and applied pale base makeup and dark red lipstick. The theater department had most of the stuff she needed, though the earrings came from the last of the markdowns in the depleted Halloween aisle at Walmart.

Singing along to the soundtrack from *Twilight* on the way to Philly, Abby strictly observed the speed limit, which wasn't easy sipping a caffeine-loaded diet soda and wound tighter than the elastic on her ponytail. The Google directions said that Night Fright was immediately off 95 and easy to find. Kyle had recommended it. She couldn't fathom how Kyle could know anything about Goth clubs, but his assessment seemed to be accurate. According to her web search, Night Fright was the "place to start" to "get into the Goth scene in Philadelphia." Besides, with club names like Sex Dwarf, Despondent Heaven, and Fast, Cheap, and Out of Control, Night Fright sounded like the safest bet. To date, the scariest place she'd ever been was Murphy's Pub on St. Patrick's Day, if you could call green beer scary.

When Abby pulled into Night Fright's parking lot, she found it brimming with cars. Had the full moon brought the creatures of the night out for combat? She checked her pallid face in the rearview mirror before exiting the car, and then wobbled on her dominatrix boots to the front door. The bouncer gave her a quick once-over. His Mohawk didn't budge as he nodded her in with "Well, well, another baby bat. You'll have lots of takers tonight."

Oh, great, I look like a newbie. Just what I wasn't going for. The pulsating music, which seemed to seep out of the walls, hit her chest. Did the erratic beat come from her heart or the clamoring vibes? She elbowed her way to the closest bar, where a skinhead bartender ogled her with one eye. The other eye roamed its socket like it was unattached. Eye contact could be problematic.

"Uh, do you have any nonalcoholic beer?" She directed her gaze at the bar surface, where various objects of carnal pleasure were embedded under polyurethane. Of the objects Abby could identify, the nipple clamps looked particularly painful.

"Trying to keep your blood pure, sweetheart?" The bartender leered.

"Just want my wits about me when I choose my pleasure for the evening." She winked at his good eye.

"Maybe I can help you out. What kind of pleasure are you looking for?" He lopped off the screw top on her beer and handed the bottle to her.

"I hate to sound stereotypical, but tall, dark, and handsome would do."

"Search no further." The bartender nodded to Abby's left.

She brought the beer nonchalantly to her lips, and then clunked the bottle on her tooth when she looked up at Malcolm McClellan.

"Did you follow me here?" The sight of him churned her stomach like a roto-rooter. With trembling hands, she set her bottle down.

He half smiled. "I could ask the same question." He wore a black leather jacket over his signature turtleneck.

"I told you I can take care of myself." She ran her tongue over her clunked tooth.

He framed her body with his arms, planting his hands on the bar. "Honestly, you can't, but you certainly are a determined little thing."

Heat rose in her cheeks. "And you're an annoying big thing." She looked him up and down, which made her want to hyperventilate. She gulped. "I'll do anything to help my students. I thought you were that kind of teacher, too."

"I used to be."

"But not anymore? That's a shame. There's nothing more satisfying than watching students reach their potential." *Yikes, that sounded a bit sanctimonious.*

He shrugged and then bent to her ear. "I need a lift back to Gettysburg. And isn't this serendipitous? I'll be able to accompany you home."

"How'd you get here?" She was dangerously close to his lips, which glistened in the dim light. Her scalp tingled. *Oh, great, now I'm lightheaded.* She took a deep breath.

"I have my ways."

"Well, I'm staying until I find someone for my play, so why don't you plant yourself in a corner somewhere and observe." She tried to shoo him away with a wave.

"I'm not leaving you alone in that get-up. You're asking for trouble. And take off those ridiculous earrings. You look like you're ready for trick or treat."

"I thought I looked like serious vampire bait." She fluttered her eyelashes at him, and when he returned her attempt at cute with a mesmerizing stare, she removed the spider webs from her ears. They'd been tickling her anyway.

"In that outfit, you'll end up in an alley . . . seriously drained."

Abby laughed, but then cut her humor short as she read Malcolm's intense expression. He took her elbow and turned her toward the exit. "You've got the actor for your play. We're leaving now."

Her heart kicked into overdrive as Malcolm maneuvered her out of Night Fright and directly to her car. "I'll drive," he said.

She threw him her keys, and she'd barely fastened her seatbelt before they were careening out of the parking lot. She held her breath when he merged onto 95 without checking for oncoming traffic. "Whoa, could you please slow down?"

"Yes, I could, but you don't have to worry about my driving." He looked at her. "My reflexes are incomparable."

"Yeah, but my nerves aren't." Abby squeezed her eyes shut. Then a hand warmed her thigh and a blast of heat radiated to her core.

"Relax, Abby." His hand squeezed gently.

In spite of the chilly night, beads of perspiration blossomed on Abby's forehead.

The speedometer read ninety, but he stared at her rather than the road. She pointed to the windshield. "Please, focus."

His charisma sucked her in. His aura frazzled her mind, as though her will was no longer her own. Truth be told, she was more excited than afraid. A raw hunger gnawed at her gut. "Do you know where I live?"

"We're not going there." His voice lowered. "We're going to my house."

His heated gaze scorched her nerves. *And what was that?* She could have sworn his eyes flashed a hint of red. Her heart thudded. Though a veil of fear engulfed her, she didn't want to escape. She felt drunk, but energy drinks and nonalcoholic beer didn't add up. The intoxication was his doing. Her head swam with something that seemed to radiate from him, and her heart tugged to move closer, to touch his flawless face. She also wanted to reach over and unzip his jeans. Instead, she clasped her hands in her lap. *Get a grip, Abby.* "Actually, we couldn't go to my apartment anyway. Four of my students are there. I let them use my place for a study group."

"Is there no end to what you will do for your students?"

Abby pursed her lips, and then said, "Not that I can think of."

Malcolm McClellan's antebellum farmhouse stood just beyond Gettysburg in the rolling country that skirted the battlefields. Recently, when Abby took some friends on a tour, she'd seen him riding a black horse across the broad plains that had once seen unspeakable carnage. One friend had remarked about his striking figure. Abby had to agree.

As he offered a hand to lead her to his front porch, her pulse raced. All those years of avoiding him, and now all she wanted was to be wrapped in his arms. Her eagerness surprised her, as though she'd been waiting for this, longing for it. At this rate, by the time they reached the bedroom, she'd be delirious.

The house was deathly dark inside.

"I'll light a few candles." He rounded the room and soon the glow of candlelight revealed Victorian furnishings and a mantel of Civil War photographs.

She thought her knees would give out when he took her hand and pulled her to him. She pressed herself against his broad chest. Wrapped in his arms, she tucked her head under his chin. It had been a while since she'd kissed anyone, and somehow she knew Malcolm would be an expert. Hoping she'd leave a good impression, she raised her face to his . . . and waited.

His lips were soft against hers . . . and cool. For a moment, she savored the feel of them, but then she wanted more. She took his bottom lip between her teeth and sucked gently. Her eagerness and lack of restraint were not like her.

He let out a low moan, like the weight of a hundred years had lifted from his shoulders.

She entwined her fingers in his thick hair, and then her tongue found his. She'd known it would be special, but she wasn't prepared for this. What started out as a gentle exploration ended with both of them breathless. When she came up for air, she brushed her fingers across his lips, now slightly swollen, and then touched her own. His teeth had scraped across her lips when they pulled apart, sending a jolt of electricity up her spine.

The mantel clock chimed, shifting her attention to the photographs there. As much as she didn't want to leave Malcolm's arms, the Civil War images drew her, and she slipped out of his embrace. An officer on horseback stood out. She picked up the frame, and then almost dropped it. The officer looked exactly like Malcolm. She'd recognize that steady, intense gaze anywhere, even in a Civil War uniform. She was no expert, but the uniform, horses, and setting looked awfully realistic. She sucked in a breath. With shaking hands, she replaced the frame on the mantel. She blew out her breath, and then looked at Malcolm. "I'm assuming that's your great grandfather?"

"No."

Abby looked at the photo again. "So, these are re-enactment photos, with you playing the role of a Union officer."

"No, they're vintage."

Her eyes widened. What was going on here? How could he possibly be in photographs from the 1860s? This was simply too odd, almost otherworldly. She'd never had an anxiety attack, but with Civil War images ricocheting around in her head and her pulse racing, a meltdown seemed imminent. She needed to get out of this house . . . pronto.

She backed toward the door, reaching behind her for the doorknob. "I've got an early day tomorrow. I'd best be going home." Realizing her shoulders were under her ears, she willed them down. "Rehearsal is at four o'clock." She dared one last glimpse at him. His eyes telegraphed lust, and her breath caught in her throat.

She slammed the door and teetered toward her car as quickly as she could in her stiletto boots. Sliding into the front seat, she immediately clicked the locks. She'd recently read that wearing stilettos thrusts a woman's pelvis forward, making her feel sexier. Tonight, bunny slippers would have been a better choice, because if she felt any "sexier," she'd implode. Like the Phantom of the Opera, Malcolm McClellan had some kind of power that pulled her into his vortex.

Taking a deep breath, she gripped the steering wheel and then clonked her head against it. Why was it that the first guy in forever who made her heart flutter also scared the crap out of her? She drove home on autopilot and was relieved to find her students gone when she pulled into her driveway.

She threw her purse on the couch and headed to her computer. With trembling hands, she opened her web browser and searched "vampire characteristics." She'd done this before at her office, but at that point it was about building a character for her play. Tonight, it was about comparing attributes that she hoped wouldn't match. Her heart clenched as her eyes scanned the list. It was like confirming poison ivy when you'd just trudged through the forest and your skin was on fire. Everything added up. Eyes glowing red—check. Uncanny reflexes—check. The intensity of his stare—check. The need for speed—check. Top all that off with the dead ringer photograph. And how had he gotten to the Goth club? He'd either vaporized or traveled as a bat. But the most compelling characteristic was the one that made him deadly. Vampires could mesmerize you with eye contact. Humans became putty in their hands. Maybe she wasn't attracted to Malcolm the man. Maybe his appeal was all about being a vampire.

Well, Abby, you wanted a convincing thespian. You got one. She shivered. She'd come dangerously close to surrendering to his charm. And what if she had? Would she now be a vampire? Or dead? She got up from her desk and paced her apartment until her thighs burned and her path made a rut in the old shag carpet. *Get a grip.* He was a professor. He doesn't want to expose himself. He wouldn't risk doing anything stupid. His reputation at the college was at stake. *Stake? Okay, bad choice of words.*

Wait a minute, Abby, where's your logic? She must really be exhausted. She was starting to believe this nonsense. Vampires didn't exist. No way. And worst case scenario . . . even if they did exist, Malcolm wasn't a vampire. She returned to the fang-framed, blood-dripping list that still glared from her computer. Surely, something wouldn't add up.

Scanning, scanning. Aha. Characteristic number twelve: Vampires burn in sunlight. That proved it. Malcolm had a day job. She'd seen him trekking across campus numerous times in broad daylight. Malcolm McClellan was simply a charismatic, sexy man. She'd never met anyone who came close to his magnetic charm, but he wasn't a vampire. He'd probably taken a course in hypnotism, and that accounted for the intense stare. He wasn't supernatural. In fact, she'd read that Steve Jobs used to stare people down to get what he wanted. Steve Jobs was a brilliant marketer, but no vampire.

She boiled water for tea, and while she watched the leaves steep in the glass carafe, she contemplated what she should do. Actually, the more she considered it, the more she realized how ideal the situation was. She could make this work. She'd just need to avoid eye contact. By the time she'd washed her face and brushed her teeth, she'd convinced herself that having Malcolm in her play was a distinct asset. Sure, he was the hottest guy she'd ever seen, but she'd be content with admiration from afar. She could bask in his incredible presence without getting close.

*

Way to go, Malcolm. Next time, flash your fangs. Watching Abby walk away was becoming a habit. She'd surely put two and two together. Malcolm shook his head at his stupidity. But he had to admit there was something oddly comforting about being discovered—like a murderer who'd harbored his crime for many years, and then confessed.

Sometimes he envied young vampires. They flaunted themselves as Goths, so even though they weren't "out," they could act the part. At least this play would give Malcolm the opportunity to be himself, to exercise his true nature, even if only on a stage.

For years, he'd had periods of recklessness, almost daring people to find him out. He'd flash a fang in a crowd or move too quickly in his classroom. He supposed it was a kind of death wish, retribution for abandoning Sarah those many years ago. If he hadn't taken that covert mission, he'd have known she needed him. But no, he couldn't be reached. If he'd just gotten to her in time, before she had a relapse, he could have saved her. Oh, God, he'd played this scene in his head thousands of times. Wasn't death preferable to this guilt?

It was a cardinal sin for vampires to reveal themselves to humans. If he were found out, the vampire council would inflict swift justice. Over the years, the council had evolved from an honorable forum to a group of thugs, headed by a French chancellor who'd been in the U.S. since the American Revolutionary War. It was no secret that Michel Auchamp wanted to harness Malcolm's ability to function in daylight. So far, he'd managed to stay under the council's radar.

But sometimes, particularly in the dead of night, the prospect of living forever became almost too much to bear. The loneliness and remorse would creep in like fog, leaving him longing for permanent release. He should have died in the war. But no, Sarah had died, and he would forever live with that guilt.

Maybe Abby would blow the whistle, exposing him. Or what if she guarded his secret? Which would he prefer?

Chapter Four

Malcolm trudged down Baltimore Pike, dragging feet that had been in stirrups since daybreak. He'd tethered Midnight just outside town, letting the battle-worn animal munch on grass. It was unlikely there'd be any hay left for the horse in town. Taking the last quarter mile by foot, the sheer will to let Sarah know he'd survived was the only force left in Malcolm's body.

Sorrow rose like bile in his throat as he thought about the men he'd lost that day. Through the haze of smoke and dust, he'd watched them fall like chess pieces across a board of rolling farmland. He touched his arm where a bullet had marked a clean path through flesh and muscle, nicking vessels but thankfully not hitting bone. The makeshift bandage was soaked with blood. An inch to the left, and he'd have lost the arm for sure. There was no compromise for shattered bone.

As he approached the first houses, he saw the bullet-ridden facades and the trampled gardens that only yesterday had been lush with summer roses. His heart clenched at the thought of Sarah being struck by a stray bullet, but with Caroline's house on a side street, she and her sister should not have been in immediate danger.

The acrid smell of artillery fire hung in the air, stinging his nostrils, and a thin layer of dust, stirred by passing caissons, grayed over porches that had welcomed visitors with spit-polished shine. The weight of battle that had passed through that day dented the brick streets.

Malcolm walked the three blocks to Caroline's house surrounded by an eerie silence, punctuated by moans emanating from upstairs windows. His men would not be here in town as their injuries were being treated in field hospitals. But he suspected that most of the homes and businesses throughout Gettysburg were now laden with thousands of soldier casualties. He hoped the civilians had taken to their basements when the Confederates marched through and that no one had been injured.

Before he could knock on Caroline's door, she rushed out of the house to meet him. "Malcolm, thank God you're all right." She squeezed his arm. "But you're white as a ghost."

He grimaced. "Careful, sister-in-law. I'm in one piece, but the arm's a bit sore." He looked beyond Caroline to the house. "Where's Sarah?"

"She's at the High Street school. They've turned it into a hospital. As soon as the gunfire stopped, she headed over there with a stack of sheets."

Malcolm backed down the porch steps. "Isn't that just like her?"

Carolyn nodded and wiped her hands on her apron. "Wait. I've been cooking all day. Take my soda bread with you." She ran into the house and returned with two baskets filled to the brim with her crusty loaves. "Can you carry a basket on your bad arm?" She proffered both baskets to Malcolm.

"I've fired a carbine and reined a horse with it, so I'm sure I can." Malcolm took both baskets in his good hand, and then transferred one to his injured arm. He staggered.

Caroline rushed forward to grab the basket. "Let's go there together."

They walked the two blocks to High Street. Malcolm's legs tingled with numbness, but he pressed on, anxious to see Sarah. Blood from his wound leeched into his uniform jacket like a scarlet tide. As they approached the red brick school, screams from an upstairs window signaled the unmistakable agony of an amputation.

Caroline faltered. "I don't know if I can go in. I've never been as brave as Sarah."

"Give me your basket." Malcolm held out his good arm, and she looped the basket just above his wrist. "Sit down on the steps and take some deep breaths."

Malcolm pushed open the heavy front door. Three women in the vestibule tore sheets into strips. One of them looked up at Malcolm, registering his blue uniform. "Union soldiers are on the second floor," she said.

"Does that mean that Confederates are on the first?" he asked.

The woman nodded. "It seems crazy to me that men who've been shooting at each other all day should now be united in suffering. That's the way of war, I suppose."

Malcolm handed the baskets off and took the stairs two at a time. His arm throbbed, and he had to steady himself on the landing before mounting the last few steps. His eyes scanned the room. A surgeon was sawing on a soldier's leg in an alcove at the far right. The boy, who couldn't have been more than sixteen, screamed like an Irish banshee. Sarah stood by his head, clutching his hand to her heart. She wore her drab gray riding dress, now spattered with blood.

The scene unfolded: the soldier's fearful eyes, Sarah's lips moving with words of comfort, the surgeon's furrowed brow as he doggedly set to his task. Malcolm stood frozen in admiration of his wife, so young, yet so brave. He wanted to sweep her away from this tragedy, to tell her that all would be well, but the scene here was magnified a hundredfold on the battlefield. The preamble to war may have been glorious, with great expectations, hearts afire, and strains of "When Johnny Comes Marching Home," but the reality was hell.

The surgeon finished his amputation, and another soldier would walk on a peg leg for the remainder of his days, providing his stump didn't become infected or typhoid fever didn't claim him. He'd mercifully lost consciousness from the trauma of metal on bone, and Sarah mopped his brow and smoothed the hair from his face. She returned his hand to his chest, but not before kissing it. Malcolm was certain she'd said a silent prayer for the soldier, too.

Malcolm shut his eyes and said a prayer as well. When he opened them, Sarah looked up and slowly turned her head toward him, as though they'd prayed in unison. Her eyes grew wide and her hands went to her mouth. She locked her gaze with his and stepped toward him. She reached out, and then stopped. "Please tell me you're not an apparition."

A smile curled his lips. "I may be back to haunt you, but I am no ghost."

She reached up to touch his cheek. "Thank you, Lord." She closed her eyes, and when she opened them she saw his arm, now soaked with blood. "Oh my darling, you're injured." Taking his uninjured arm in hers, she led him to a chair. When he sat, he realized it was the first time he'd done so that day.

"It's nothing, Sarah." He started to get back up, but a wave of lightheadedness hit him, and he collapsed back in the chair.

"You've lost a lot of blood," she said, "and that wound could get infected. At least let the doctor have a look at it."

"I'm fine. " He struggled to get up, and then the room began spinning and his world went black.

Chapter Five

Abby and Kyle sat in the first row of the theater, mapping out the blocking for scene two. The supporting cast sat behind them.

"I'm just going to observe today," Kyle said.

Oh, great.

Abby sensed Malcolm's presence before she saw him, like static in the air before a lightning strike. The hair on her arms stood up, and she jerked her head toward the theater entrance. Her heartbeat sped up. *Stay neutral.* She'd successfully blocked him from her thoughts, but being in his presence posed a challenge.

"I think we're all here now." Abby looked back at the papers on her lap, determined not to make eye contact with Malcolm. She shot a glance at Kyle, who frowned at her.

"Let's get started." Kyle rose to shake Malcolm's hand. "Whoa, your hand is cold. Getting a bit chilly out there, is it?"

"More like a heat wave," Abby said under her breath. *Vampires' skin is cool to the touch—check.*

"What was that?" Malcolm asked.

Vampires have exceptional hearing—check. She glanced in his direction, and her eyes made it as far as his crotch. *Exceptional everything.* "Nothing, just babbling." She pushed herself out of the chair, took the stage steps two at a time, and then turned to face Malcolm, Kyle, and the rest of the cast.

"Good afternoon, everyone. I want to personally thank you all for participating in our annual holiday production. It's always an exciting day when the tryouts are over, and the full cast assembles for the first time. I'd especially like to welcome Dr. Malcolm McClellan to the cast. He's *graciously* accepted the role of our vampire hero. I'm sure his experience as a Civil War re-enactor

33

will serve us well as we steep ourselves in the history of those tragic days that put little Gettysburg indelibly on the map." *Okay, now I sound like a chamber of commerce brochure.*

"Anyway, enough of that. You all have your scripts, and to begin, I'll need Dr. McClellan and Karen Thompson on stage, please." Abby watched Malcolm take Karen's elbow to help her up the steps. Her breath caught. *No, couldn't be jealousy. He just doesn't want her to trip.*

"Karen, you stand here." Abby pointed to the yellow chalk marks on the floor to her left. She adjusted Karen's stance by moving her shoulders so that her body angled about 45 degrees toward the audience. "Dr. McClellan, if you'll take the same stance?"

"I don't see what you're intending, Miss Potter," Malcolm said.

Abby looked up at him. *Wow.* She almost fainted when she met his eyes. That color blue didn't exist anywhere else in nature. She cleared her throat, and then said, "What's so difficult? Just stand at the same angle I placed Karen."

"Show me."

Damn, he wasn't making this easy. She stood next to him, facing Karen, and turned her shoulders halfway toward the front of the stage. "Got it?" She didn't look up at him this time.

"Not quite."

This was getting ridiculous. She firmly grasped his shoulders. "Like this." She moved him about three inches, and then let her eyes travel from his broad chest up to his cleft chin. She stopped at his lips. Her body leaned toward him, and then she jerked back. "I'm going to sit down, now. I'll cue you from the front row." As she walked away, her heart mimicked a microwaved marshmallow— after an explosive puff, it quickly deflated.

Abby eased her jittery body into a front row seat and flipped open her script. "Let's start on page three. We'll do a quick read through for timing and inflection. Dr. McClellan, whenever you're ready."

She sat for a few minutes and then, as was her custom, got up and roamed the theater, making sure the actors could be heard from all the nooks and crannies. Malcolm far exceeded amateur status. He read like a seasoned professional. His projection was pitch-perfect, and though his baritone could have easily drowned out Karen, he seemed to modulate his volume to bring out the best in hers. Abby thought back to his classroom. He'd always found a way to let his students shine. If they seemed stuck on a question, he'd reword it to encourage their answer. Abby stared at him in admiration—the same kind of admiration that had engendered a schoolgirl crush when she'd been a student. And for a moment, she forgot he might be anything more than mortal. She only saw the man, his self-confidence, his ability to make those around him comfortable. Even though he was capable of overshadowing anyone, he'd checked his ego at the door. He didn't need to put on airs, and *that* was a tremendous turn-on.

*

After one hundred fifty years of solitude, why was he suddenly lonelier than he'd ever been? The window of his heart had only opened a crack, and yet Abby had invaded it like a monsoon. Watching her take command of the play made him proud of the capable woman she'd become. It also made him recall his life with Sarah and how he'd failed her.

Sarah. The years had dulled his pain, and Abby had rekindled his passion. But that was his human side, the side that crushed his first attempt at love. What made him think he deserved another?

Better to stick with his vampire nature, ruled by more basic instincts.

Returning to his empty house following rehearsal, he headed to the kitchen and poured himself a tumbler of B positive, first inhaling the spicy scent of the rich red liquid, and then swishing it around in his mouth before swallowing. He wondered how Abby's blood would taste. Even if she came to him, wanted him, he'd have to keep his impulses in check. He could make love to her without sinking his fangs in her neck, but it wouldn't be easy. And if he bit her, could he stop his onslaught . . . before he turned her . . . or killed her? He hadn't tasted blood fresh from a vein in more than a century. Such temptation.

Chapter Six

After the cast left for the evening, Kyle loped around the empty stage, too pent up to sit. Over the past two years, since his first introduction to the Night Fright vampires, named after the club where they worked, he'd learned to control his trembling. He still agonized about what mood they'd be in. A lot depended on how frequently they'd fed. There were times he thought they'd just as soon drain him as enlist him.

The three vamps dropped silently, one by one, from the theater's rafters, and Kyle stiffened. Before they had a chance to grill him, he said, "Abby played right into my hands. She fell for the Malcolm McClellan ploy . . . hook, line, and sinker."

Arlo, who generally served as the spokesperson for the vamps—spokevamp?—said, "No surprise there. He's the prototype of the archaic, duty-bound vamp, exactly the kind we're trying to obliterate." He worked his tongue like a serpent, flicking it rapidly. The notion of obliteration had obviously excited him.

"Cool," Kyle said. "We've come a long way since I gave you guys a tour of the campus two years ago. Who'd have thought we'd get so tight?"

Arlo smacked his lips and nodded at his compatriots. "Yes, you were very helpful, pointing out the vulnerable coeds. I can still taste the blood of that sweet little freshman. She was tantalizing." Kyle could have sworn Arlo's tongue was forked as he licked his lips.

"That was my point of no return," Kyle said. "The terror in her eyes was the biggest turn on I'd ever experienced." It induced a yearning in him to abandon his humanity and join their ranks.

"Yes, and here we are—close to our goal." Arlo smiled. "Once Malcolm's dust, we'll turn you."

"I've always believed vampires were real, but I sure didn't suspect Malcolm McClellan was one," Kyle said, shaking his head. "How could a vampire function in daylight?"

"That's why we want him," Arlo said.

Sometimes Kyle wondered if the other two Night Fright boys could even talk, but he'd once seen Arlo clip the platinum blonde one on the head for opening his mouth, so he figured they were cautious.

"Only a handful of vampires in history have possessed the ability to not burn in sunlight, but unfortunately, they've been an honorable lot. They could have shared their unique genetic code by creating more vampires, but they won't doom humans to their fate except under dire circumstances . . . or because of love. The vampire council has attempted to harness their trait for centuries. Imagine how we could mainstream." Arlo paced the stage, gesturing in sweeping arm movements. "If any of these vamps had been willing to surrender just a few vials of their blood, the council could have already created an army of daylight vamps."

"I don't get why you haven't just grabbed him, tied him down, stuck a needle in his arm and taken some blood," Kyle said.

"The council had hoped to find a vamp willing to share, but over the years, the vamps with that specific genetic code have dispersed throughout the world. It's all come back to Malcolm," Arlo said. "And now we're delightfully close. It's ideal, really—a vampire playing a vampire. Malcolm won't be able to resist displaying some vampire characteristics on stage, and that's all the proof the council will need. Just a flash of fang or display of red eyes will be enough for the council to nab him."

"And just to help things along, I thought I'd get the cast together for one of Gettysburg's famous ghost tours. Sort of loosen things up a bit," Kyle said.

"Brilliant idea," said Arlo. "The more comfortable Malcolm becomes in his role as a vampire, the more likely he'll be to let his guard down."

Arlo signaled to the other Night Fright boys, and without so much as a wave goodbye, they flew back up to the rafters. Kyle assumed they would morph to bat form and exit through an eave.

The winter chill permeated the old theater, and Kyle rubbed his arms to dispel his goose bumps. He chuckled to himself. When he became a vampire, he wouldn't have to worry about severe Pennsylvania winters. He'd be immune to heat and cold. It couldn't happen fast enough for him. Once they drained and decapitated Malcolm, they promised Kyle he could join their ranks.

The Night Fright boys would be lurking in corners tomorrow evening, no doubt salivating over some of the cute coeds. Damn, he couldn't wait to be lurking with them, and now his dreams were within his grasp.

*

Of all the idiotic plans Malcolm had to endure from humans, attending a ghost tour would have been at the top of the list. Close proximity to a group of humans whose blood would be pumping wildly from the excitement of the tour, and thus making him salivate, would only be trumped by the lame and inaccurate stories about ghosts in Gettysburg. He'd heard the guides embellished the tall tales per the enthusiasm of the crowd. And this crowd of thespians would surely be enthusiastic. He'd be biting his tongue to keep from correcting the flubs. Flubs? That was a word Abby would use. He smiled. Maybe the tour wouldn't be so bad. Perhaps he could comfort her if she squealed from fear. He'd wrap her in his arms and press her head to his chest. Her hair smelled like the sweet peas in his mother's garden. Malcolm scrubbed a hand across his eyes. *Stop these nonsensical thoughts.*

When he arrived at Ghost Tours of Gettysburg, which assembled at the Best Western Gettysburg Hotel, he learned that their group would be taking the "extreme" tour. *By all means, kick it up a notch.* This tour would meander through town and end at Gettysburg Cemetery, where Lincoln had delivered his Gettysburg Address. Bite his tongue? Add smoke pouring from his ears.

The rest of the cast trickled in, though Abby was still absent. They assembled in front of the Best Western, all of them puffing the winter air and hopping with the chill. Malcolm stood stone still. He could put up a front of minding the cold, but he was too irritated by the situation to play along. Until he saw Abby, and his icy mood thawed.

"Sorry I'm late." She joined the hopping crowd. Her breasts bounced. *Lovely.*

When Kyle arrived, his eyes darted around Lincoln Square in front of the hotel.

"We're all here," Abby said. "We just need our tour guide."

And wouldn't you know, sweeping around the corner in head-to-toe black came the inimitable Miss Fontaine, Gettysburg's mistress of the supernatural. She'd written a widely distributed pamphlet on Gettysburg ghosts that made Malcolm gag. Sarah's sister, Caroline, was one of her featured stories. Thank God she hadn't written about Malcolm and Sarah. He couldn't have endured that.

"Well, citizens," Miss Fontaine began, "thank you for joining me this evening." She cupped a hand to her ear. "I can hear you ruminating. You're wondering what I have in store. Well, well, well. Don't be tortured by uncertain wonders. I'm here to share a passel of memories. You see, I was in Gettysburg on those fateful three days that changed our fair city. I was, in fact, pressed into service by the Union Army as a spy." She swept an arm around the square. "I witnessed the seeds of our destruction being sowed, but that's neither here nor someplace else." She clapped her hands. "Time to quit this square."

Miss Fontaine held a closed umbrella in the air and pointed it to the south. "We shall commence to the graveyard by way of Mrs. Caroline Foster's house."

Oh, God, no. Malcolm had avoided the house where Sarah died for more than a hundred years. Would he ever get past his sorrow and guilt? He swallowed the lump in his throat. Damn his human feelings.

"Will we be going to the Dobbins House?" Kyle asked.

"I haven't decided that to a definite aim," Miss Fontaine said, "but I reckon you all can stop there after the cemetery. I don't typically go through the woods, though it being winter and all, there won't be copperheads performing misdeeds." She motioned for the group to follow her.

Malcolm was actually impressed with Miss Fontaine's Civil War aphorisms. At least there was some amusement in this wretched excursion. And observing Abby, he could long for her, not that that was a good thing. He stayed at the back of the group as they meandered past downtown Gettysburg's storefronts, though he could hear her conversation.

"Why do you want to go to the Dobbins House?" Abby nudged Kyle.

"Oh, a couple of my friends are going to be there, and I thought I'd meet up with them."

"You're kind of jumpy tonight," Abby said.

"Who me? Nah." Kyle stumbled off the curb.

Abby shook her head.

Needing a distraction, Malcolm caught up with Abby and steered her to the front of the group. "I thought you might enjoy some historical facts as we go along. Facts being the operative word."

"What, Miss Fontaine isn't accurate enough for you?" She looked up at him. "She's sure got the lingo down."

"Yes, I'll give her that, but there were no recorded female spies in Gettysburg."

"So, her credibility did an abrupt nosedive with you, eh?" Abby chuckled.

God, she was appealing when she laughed. He wanted to suck on her bottom lip.

"Miss Fontaine is entertaining, and as long as she doesn't butcher the facts too badly, I should be able to keep my mouth shut," Malcolm said.

"Shall I pinch you if you get out of line?"

"You can do more than pinch me."

Simultaneously, they stopped and faced each other. The rest of the group walked around them to keep up with Miss Fontaine, leaving Abby and Malcolm standing under one of the city's vintage streetlamps.

"Malcolm, I don't know what kind of power you have over me, but it's making me very uncomfortable." She crossed her arms . . . under her breasts.

"You're the one who suggested a pinch."

"I know, but I'm not myself when I'm around you. God knows what I'll say next."

"How about 'Would you like to bite my neck?'"

"What?" Abby backed up, clutching her throat. She stopped when she smacked the window of the florist shop. She stared at Malcolm in horror. "That's not funny."

He raked a hand through his hair. He had repressed the human feelings surrounding his grief for Sarah. In their place, his vampire lust had risen to the surface. "Sorry, bad joke. I'm getting a bit carried away with this role I'm playing. Let's join the others." He offered his hand, but Abby didn't take it. Instead, she sprinted to catch up with the group.

Again, nice move, Malcolm. Abby talked about the power he had over her, but it was the other way around. She had the power. If she wanted, she could bring him to his knees. And she had no idea. He purposefully lagged behind. He didn't want to hear what Miss Fontaine had to say about his sister-in-law, but when he caught up with the group at the Foster residence, she'd just begun her dissertation.

"I am much obliged to the current owners of this home," Miss Fontaine said as she herded the group on the expansive front porch of the Foster homestead. "Since this is a private residence, we won't go inside, but they graciously allow us to congregate here on the porch where Caroline Foster used to cool the pies and Irish soda bread she provided to the hospitals following the Battle of Gettysburg."

At least she got that right.

"Gather around. I'd like to read a letter written by Caroline Foster. Her sister, Sarah, died in this house, and hers is the spirit that still roams this property at eventide."

Malcolm stiffened. He was stuck with this band of humans and his damn grief.

"This letter was written to Caroline's kin in Harrisburg. The original is in a museum there, but I was privileged to obtain a copy. It begins 'I have no news since first frost of the year past. My dear brother-in-law, Malcolm, is still missing, and I may only presume that he died during the final days in Virginia. I believe his will to live departed when Sarah died. We have all suffered as a result of this terrible conflict. I was glad to hear that your daughter and her beau are intended, and I hope to get there to see them rightly married. Your cousin, Caroline.'"

Malcolm stole a glance at Abby, who stared at him, wide-eyed. She opened her mouth, and then shut it. She cleared her throat, and then in a hoarse whisper said, "Perhaps Dr. McClellan can expand on the history of this family."

"Not I," Malcolm said quickly. His eyes didn't leave Abby's.

"We can't tarry," Miss Fontaine interjected. "The graveyard awaits." She probably wasn't interested in anyone else's account anyway. Heaven forbid someone should prove her wrong, and that someone would *not* be Malcolm.

"Excellent idea," Malcolm said. Miss Fontaine was dead wrong about one thing. Sarah's spirit did not roam this house. If it did, Malcolm was sure he'd be able to sense it. It didn't make him any less sad, however. Hearing Caroline's letter flooded his heart with painful memories. He needed to get away from this house. Leaping off the porch, he headed for the street.

"Uh, excuse me," Miss Fontaine shouted after him. "We're going through the rose garden first."

Over his shoulder, Malcolm said, "I'm not. I'll join you at the cemetery." He couldn't bear to see the garden Sarah had cultivated for her sister, nor the bench Caroline had added in memory of Sarah. With long strides, he rounded the corner back to Baltimore Pike. This was idiocy . . . the play . . . those horrible memories . . . Abby. He picked up his pace.

Abby wanted to catch up with Malcolm, but what would she say? That Foster house had obviously rattled him. When Miss Fontaine read Caroline's letter, he froze. It was as though the letter was about him. Her knees buckled, and she stopped to catch her breath. Wait, she'd been down this train of thought before. The Malcolm she knew couldn't have been alive in 1860. He didn't look a day over thirty-five, so how could he be one hundred and fifty? Of course, since she'd been his student, he hadn't aged a day. Vampires didn't age. *Stop it, Abby.*

And what was up with Kyle? This ghost tour had been his idea, but he was sure acting nervous. He couldn't be taking this stuff seriously. Anyway, Miss Fontaine's spiel was more entertaining than spooky.

Abby stayed in the back of the group. The four-block walk to the cemetery took them outside the parameters of downtown, and Miss Fontaine passed out flashlights as they neared the black wrought-iron gates. This place was eerie in the daylight, but tonight a dense fog blanketed the rolling hills, making visibility negligible. The flashlights created weird patterns through the fog, almost like ghosts rising from the graves.

As she caught up with everyone, Malcolm stood by a tall gravestone, peering across the vast graveyard. The corners of his mouth turned down in a sorrowful expression, and Abby's heart ached for him. Her parents had told her she had too much sympathy. Both doctors, they said she'd need to toughen up if she expected to follow in their footsteps. Medicine had been her original dream . . . until she'd taken a class from Malcolm McClellan, and she veered to teaching. But the pain that swelled in her heart for Malcolm was more than sympathy. It was empathy. She grieved with him. Damn. This ghost tour was turning out to be a very bad idea indeed.

She looked at Kyle, who was blowing on his fingers. She could strangle him for suggesting this stupid tour. He didn't even seem to be enjoying it.

Miss Fontaine droned on and on about various markers and how flowers disappeared on graves and then magically appeared again. Yada yada.

Malcolm meandered through the markers, stopping at a few, but not seeming engaged. He wore a blank expression, which was an improvement over his sorrowful one. A wave of relief washed over Abby's heart.

Now that Malcolm had calmed, Abby's attention turned to the plummeting temperature. She didn't want to appear rude, but her toes were numb in her sheepskin boots, and she could sure use a beer. She nudged Kyle, who took the hint.

When Miss Fontaine paused, Kyle interjected, "If you don't mind, Miss Fontaine, we're going to peel off and head to Dobbins for a brew. It's been enlightening . . . and loads of fun." He applauded, and the group followed suit. "Thanks so much."

"Thank *you*," Abby whispered under her breath to Kyle. "One more ghost anecdote, and I may have puked."

"Don't puke yet. Not until you've gotten a few ales under your belt, at least."

Ordinarily, Kyle would have jabbed her in the ribs and laughed with a comment like that, but he just headed off to the exit gate. Weird.

Dobbins Tavern was crowded as usual. For a raucous time, you couldn't beat the old tavern. It was housed in Gettysburg's oldest, most historic home. Abby loved the beamed ceilings, bookcases, and cozy atmosphere of the place. And tonight, the fireplaces would definitely be appreciated. The old house had played a role during the Civil War, harboring slaves on their journey to freedom. Abby headed straight for one of the fireplaces and began warming her hands over the glowing embers. Though she wanted to search the group for Malcolm, she resisted. Before she'd had a chance to order, Kyle brought her a tankard.

"Porter, correct?" He handed her the brew.

"Perfect." She sipped. "Are you all right?"

"Yeah, fine. "

He didn't look fine. "Okay, whatever you say." Abby turned back to the fireplace, and then a hand circled her waist. She jumped when she looked up at the face of the bartender from Night Fright. She'd have recognized that wall-eyed glare anywhere.

"Whoa, where'd you come from?" She looked from the bartender to Kyle, who grinned.

"This is my friend, Arlo," Kyle said, clipping Arlo on the shoulder.

"You're kidding. I mean, really?" Abby backed away from Arlo's chummy hand. "Why didn't you tell me you had a friend at Night Fright when I went to Philly?"

"What, and spoil the fun for independent you?" Kyle chuckled. "Arlo and a couple of his cohorts will be hanging around the theater to keep an eye on our star. Make sure his portrayal is authentic."

"I suppose he sees his share of vampire wannabes." Abby looked sideways at Arlo. "Mighty accommodating of you."

"Where is our star?" Arlo asked.

Abby scanned the dark tavern, but Malcolm was nowhere in sight. "He must have peeled off after the cemetery." Abby chugged her tankard, and then she slapped her thigh. "I think I'll head out." She started to hold out a hand to shake Arlo's, and then thought better of it, scratching her nose instead.

"Nice to see you again," Arlo said. He half grinned.

As Abby left the tavern, the tour guide's words played in her head. That letter she'd read, with the soldier named Malcolm, had punched Abby in the gut. Of course, Malcolm was an old-fashioned name, and in the nineteenth century, it was used more prevalently than today, but as Abby recalled the Civil War photographs on Malcolm's mantel, a shiver that wasn't due to the cold temperature rose up her spine. Had he really been a Union soldier? She shook her head. Nonsense.

Chapter Seven

Sarah stroked Malcolm's uninjured arm. He hadn't regained consciousness since collapsing in her arms.

Dr. Hayes patted Sarah's back. "He'll be better off resting at home than here," he said. The doctor had bathed and bandaged Malcolm's wound, which had finally stopped bleeding.

"He seems to have lost a lot of blood." Sarah frowned.

Dr. Hayes shook his head. "Yes, more than he should have with this type of wound. A few vessels were clipped, but I thought I'd never stop the bleeding. Does he bruise easily?"

"He frequently has bruises, but he's a very physical man, doctor. Isn't that common for someone who works with horses?"

"It's a matter of degrees, Mrs. McClellan. I suspect his blood is thin, and he's certainly lost quite a bit of it." Dr. Hayes wiped his brow with the back of his hand. "What he needs is rest. Take him home, and when he rallies, try to get some soup down him." He put a hand on Sarah's shoulder. "Can you and your sister carry him in a stretcher? I can't spare anyone here."

"Of course we can carry him."

*

Malcolm didn't remember the journey back to Caroline's house, and he drifted in and out of consciousness for several days. It seemed that every time he woke up, Sarah was there with a spoonful of soup. By the third day, he was able to sit up and take some soup by himself. "I need to get back to my regiment," he said to Sarah as she sat in a rocking chair, mending his uniform.

"I knew you'd say that as soon as you could talk." She smiled at him. "But General Lee has retreated, and I'm sure you'll hear from your superiors soon enough. They only have so many colonels to spare."

Two more days passed, and Malcolm was able to take short walks around the house. Following one such excursion, he noticed that Sarah eyed him provocatively as he returned to bed. She set the mending on her sewing basket, got up from the rocker, and walked slowly to their bed. Sitting gently on the edge, she took Malcolm's hand. "Before I let you go back to the saddle, I need to make sure you're fit to ride."

"And how do you propose to do that?" Malcolm gave her an expectant grin.

Sarah crept onto the bed, and then stood, straddling Malcolm's legs. With hands on hips, she swayed back and forth. She fisted a hunk of skirt and slowly began hiking up the calico material, revealing shapely ankles. She swished the skirt around her legs as the material inched up her calves. She teased him with her knees, first showing a glimpse, and then quickly covering them. The next time her skirts rose above her knees, she pulled higher, to her thighs.

Malcolm gasped, and she giggled.

She eased the material up her thighs, revealing a complete lack of undergarments and the lush curls hiding her treasure. Laughing, and then falling to her knees, she knee-walked to his thighs. She fiddled with the drawstring on his drawers, and then stopped. "Please tell me to stop if you're not feeling up to this."

"I believe you'll find I'm quite up to it." He glanced down at the decided tent in his pants.

She took the book from his hands and tossed it on the floor. Tugging on his drawstring, she loosed his engorged manhood and began stroking the considerable length of it with one hand while with the other, she pulled the ribbon at the neck of her gown.

"Here, let me help with that. You already have your hands full." He separated the muslin bodice, flimsy from many washings, and traced her tender nipples with his calloused thumbs.

She closed her eyes and adjusted her hips. Placing the tip of him at her bud, she dipped him briefly inside to taste the honey of her sheath, and then withdrew him to circle the epicenter of her pleasure.

"Put me inside you," Malcolm said, his voice rough. He moved a hand to her feminine folds and caressed her bud with his thumb.

She slipped him inside, but drew back when the depth of his thrusts became too deep. "In this position, you're a touch too big for me."

"You're small inside," Malcolm said, "and I love how tight you hold me there, but I never want to hurt you." He gripped her hips and moved her slightly back, where he could continue to thrust without bumping the entrance to her womb. "Is that better?"

"Yes." She opened her eyes. "Now, no more talking." Sarah focused on Malcolm's lips, which were slightly parted. His blue eyes blazed as his breathing hastened to a jagged rhythm, matching his thrusts. He closed his eyes and gripped her buttocks. His arms flexed against her and his fingers dug into her flesh. When he came, the explosion of his climax sent sparks of warmth and power through Sarah's limbs.

Malcolm pulled Sarah down to him and wrapped his arms around her. He whispered in her hair, "Sarah, Sarah. I lose myself in you."

Chapter Eight

Malcolm drummed the eraser of his pencil on his leather desk blotter and watched a bank of melting ice plummet from the roof outside his office. Something about the finality of that thud as the ice shattered on the balcony reminded him of his heart. Damn. Hadn't he figured out how to live in the human world? One hundred and fifty years of peace and solitude had served him well. Then Abby had sauntered into his office and fixed him with those hazel eyes.

What was it about this woman? He was used to come-ons from coeds and colleagues, and he was impervious. When he'd lost Sarah, he put his heart into cold storage. Memories of her surfaced unexpectedly when the scent of the lilacs she'd planted sweetened his property in the spring or when a new student roll listed a coed named Sarah. He'd allow himself a brief moment to savor the recollection of her body under his. That lovely memory was usually chased by a hammering guilt and grief, and he'd dive back to his seclusion. With Abby's appearance, the closed chamber of his heart released a feeling he hadn't experienced since the nineteenth century—hope.

Like the first time he'd seen Sarah, when she flirted with him at the Harvest Ball, Abby held the promise of good things to come. He remembered when she'd been his student and the day she'd come to his office, just when he'd hit his lowest ebb. He was so struck by her sincerity when she'd told him how he'd inspired her that he couldn't even think of a reply. Inspiring? Not an adjective he'd use to describe himself. Not anymore. He'd lapsed into a life of endless gray, and his students all had the same face. Abby was a woman who saw possibilities at every turn. He rarely thought beyond the next exam;

she envisioned her students on graduation day, proudly accepting their diplomas and making their way in the world.

And then there was the matter of her body, soft and supple as south Indian silk. He massaged his temples. *Leave her alone, you fool.*

*

"Abby, did you hear me?" Kyle waved his hands in front of her.

"Huh? Oh, yeah, you asked about costumes?" Abby shook her head from thoughts of Malcolm—for about the hundredth time that day.

"Go check the FedEx deliveries. We should have received that taffeta you ordered."

"Oh, right. I mean, absolutely. I'll get on that." She backed out of Kyle's office while he shook his head at her.

"We're on a very tight deadline, Abs. I shouldn't have to tell you that."

"I know. I'm sorry. Just a bit distracted today." She closed the door behind her and took a deep breath before considering her next destination . . . the campus post office.

Distracted? No shit.

This called for some brain thrashing. Exhibit A: Garden-variety woman. Exhibit B: Superman . . . and possibly something else. *No, don't go there. Where's your common sense? Wake up, Abby.* Her fascination with Malcolm would probably fade when she didn't have to see him every day. Once the play was over, he'd retreat to his reclusive lifestyle, and she could go back to thinking about the next production. And what were Kyle and his creepy crony up to? Making sure Malcolm's portrayal was authentic? Seemed mighty odd.

Let's just get past this play.

Stepping up her pace, she arrived at the post office, picked up the parcels of material that had arrived from New York and rushed to the costume mistress across town. Mental note: set up sewing machine at home for last-minute alterations. She checked her watch, two p.m. She'd have just enough time to visit Pat, and then grab a veggie burger before the four p.m. rehearsal.

Patricia Wiggins, the best seamstress Abby had ever known, was leaning against the open door to her shop, Retro Mania, when Abby approached. The shop specialized in vintage clothing, costuming, and alterations. She was smoking a cigarette through a long black holder . . . à la Holly Golightly, though that's where the resemblance stopped. Patricia was more zaftig than svelte. And her clothes were recycled gypsy, flowing, gauzy fabrics sprinkled with tiny bells that tinkled when she moved. Her wrist-to-elbow arm bangles would have weighed down a smaller woman. Everyone said Patricia *was* a gypsy, and some even called her a witch because she had a little fortune-telling slash séance business on the side, but Abby just thought she was highly intuitive. Over the years, she'd asked Pat for advice more than a few times, and the clairvoyant woman had always come through with profound insights.

"Hey, lady." Abby kissed Pat on the cheek. "I brought the material for you to do your magic. Sorry it's so late, and as you know, we're on a tight deadline."

"No problem. I can always use *real* magic to help me with the straight seams. I've almost mastered set-in sleeves, but I think I used one too many spider legs the last time I tried. I ended up with so little give that I had to recycle the sleeves as jock straps." She chuckled. "I'm just kidding."

"I never know when to take you seriously." Abby didn't laugh.

"What's with the long face?" Patricia motioned for Abby to enter her shop, where Pat's three black felines played hide and seek among racks of jewel-toned costumes.

"Sorry. I've got the weight of the world on my shoulders."

"Wouldn't have anything to do with that hunk of a professor, would it?"

Abby froze in her tracks. "Geez, Pat, does nothing escape you?"

"I keep tabs on the people I care about, and for better or worse, you're one." She put her arm around Abby's shoulders. "Tell me if you want me to butt out. I know you had to bring me the material, but I was going to get in touch with you today, anyway."

"I could use some advice." Abby thawed enough to plop on Patricia's overstuffed loveseat, which rested inside a canopy of palm trees at the back of Pat's shop. Abby never understood how Pat could grow palms inside, without natural sunlight, in non-tropical Pennsylvania, but Pat and her shop embodied quirks and mysteries.

Pat sat next to Abby and took her hand. She closed her eyes, paused, and then began speaking with her eyes still shut. "Promise me you won't freak out." She peeked at Abby with one eye.

"I promise, and believe me, I'm already beyond freaking out."

"All right." She patted Abby's hand. "Here's what you need to know." She took a deep breath and blew it out through puffed cheeks. "Malcolm McClellan is not exactly of this world, but you can trust him."

"Oh, geez, I've been driving myself crazy." Abby's pressed her hand to her heart. "Is he really, truly what I think he might be?"

Pat looked sideways at Abby. "What do you think he might be?"

Abby chewed on her lip. Her lungs constricted, and she thumped her chest with her fist to get the words out. "I've got stacks of research that point to him being something besides human, but there's one characteristic that doesn't line up."

Pat grimaced. "You mean the one about tolerating daylight?"

Staring wide-eyed at Pat, Abby said, "All right, fill me in." She slumped back into the loveseat and gripped the padded armrests. "I've been wrestling with myself ever since I saw those vintage photos at his house. And then on the ghost tour, our guide read an old letter that mentioned a soldier named Malcolm in the Civil War. It gave me chills. The truth is, my one thread of hope has been the daylight thing."

"Not to dash your hopes, my dear, but some creatures of the night have special abilities."

"Oh, criminy." Abby squeezed her eyes shut, and then had to force them open to look at Pat. "He's a vampire."

Pat nodded. "I'm afraid so, but it's not the end of the world. You have feelings for him, don't you?"

"Oh, God, right now I don't know what I'm feeling." Abby threw up her hands. "I've always been attracted to him, but when I thought he might be, you know, a vampire—" she grimaced, "—I just didn't see how that could compute." She clutched her throat. "As a fantasy, the neck-biting stuff is kind of romantic, but in reality, it totally creeps me out. Besides, I've never believed in anything paranormal."

She squinted at Pat. "However, all these years I knew there was something special about *you*. Every time you've told me something was going to happen, it did. Like the time I got the lead in *Our Town*, in spite of Pamela Shields trying to sabotage me. You warned me about that."

"I didn't know specifically what she was going to do, but I knew she was up to no good." Pat screwed up her nose. "And that's another thing. I hate to have to tell you, but Miss Shields is back in Gettysburg."

Abby sat up straight as a poker stick. "Why?"

"She wants your job."

"Super. Just what I need." Abby rolled her eyes. "I'll have to make sure the theater's locked up when we're not rehearsing. She's been known to steal things. When my dress disappeared from wardrobe the day before the *Our Town* opening, I knew Pamela was the culprit."

"She'll be looking for ways to trip you up, so be very careful." Pat screwed up her nose. "And that's not all. Don't trust Kyle. Those goons from Night Fright are vampires, and they're after Malcolm."

"What?" Abby threw up her hands, and then she got up from the loveseat and started pacing. "Has the whole world gone crazy?"

"No, but your little corner is hell-bent for leather. Look, I'm sorry I put you on anguish overload. Don't worry too much about Pamela or Kyle now. I've got my eye on them, and you've got enough to digest sorting out your feelings for Malcolm."

Abby shivered, violently. She'd maintained her cool for as long as she could, and suddenly the reality of Pat's news came crashing down like an old theater set. *Oh, God's green earth.* Her hand went to her mouth, and she raced to Pat's bathroom, where she barely made it to the toilet. She spewed the remnants of her breakfast. When she thought the stomach upheaval was done, she splashed water on her face and stared in the mirror. *Malcolm really is a vampire. Vampires really do exist.* Terrified, she had to return to the bowl for another round. This time, she didn't look at herself in the mirror after she cleaned up.

Taking baby steps, she returned to Pat, who held out a ginger ale.

"Thanks," Abby said shakily.

Pat wrapped her arms around Abby. "Would you like a tension tamer?"

"Like Xanax?"

"No, just my homeopathic concoction."

"I'd love one, but I'd better not. I need to get back to work." Abby blinked hard.

"Well, try not to worry. I'm here for you whenever you need me. There's a lot more to this world than meets the untrained eye. I'll help you understand it."

"Thanks, Pat." Abby chewed on her lip.

"And while you're getting used to the idea of the man you care about being a vampire, remember that feelings don't lie. And don't try to intellectualize the situation, just feel it."

Abby headed back to the theater, her mind racing. She wouldn't detour for a veggie burger now. Just the thought of food made her gag. So many conflicting thoughts bombarded her brain. Yes, she was attracted to Malcolm, and Pat said he was trustworthy, but in her heart of hearts, she already knew that. The fact that he was a vampire was creepy beyond belief, but that wasn't what bothered her most. No, the main issue was this man who had kept his identity hidden for who knows how long was now on a stage acting out his base nature. What would that do to him, and would the audience pick up on his otherworldly ways? Maybe it was her protective nature, but more than any other feeling that swelled in her heart, she feared for him.

Chapter Nine

If Abby thought she'd been doing everything she could to avoid Malcolm, he seemed to be doing even more to avoid her. After a week of rehearsal, not only was he not looking at her, but he didn't seem to hear anything she said. He was directing himself. Today after rehearsal, she'd remind him who was supposed to be directing whom.

But rehearsal didn't go as she'd planned.

Abby heard the theater door open behind her, but she didn't turn around to look. She figured a few students had entered the theater to watch their friends rehearse. Not until she took the stage to bring Karen her parasol did she get a view of the audience. Sitting a few rows from the front was Pamela Shields. She and Pamela had been rivals for a number of theatrical roles when they were students, and the last Abby knew, Pamela was designing sets in New York. Though Pamela was talented, her temper could flare, and when it did, anyone within shouting distance got the brunt of it. And now, Pamela had returned to Gettysburg to usurp Abby's job. *Terrific.*

Having Pamela there was enough of a downer, but then Abby spied additional intruders in the last row of the theater. She couldn't make out their faces, but three sets of eyes glowed red in the dark. *Oh, shit.* She looked at Malcolm, whose flared nostrils told her that he'd seen them, too.

"GO AWAY." Malcolm's voice bounced off the walls.

Everyone in the theater looked to the rear where the intruders rose simultaneously from their seats. They moved so fast to exit the theater, their forms left blurry streaks.

Karen and Pamela screamed. Abby froze, and then glanced around to gauge reactions. The consensus was slack jaws and a lot of blinking. Except for Kyle, who wore a Cheshire cat smile.

Abby looked quickly at Malcolm, fists clenched at his side.

"I think we're all so exhausted from rehearsal that we're seeing things," she said, laughing. "I could have sworn I saw something fly across the stage a minute ago."

All eyes jerked to the stage. All except Malcolm's, who stared at her.

"Okay, I think that's enough fun for today," Abby announced.

Still smiling, Kyle said, "Fine, let's wrap."

Abby didn't wait for anyone else to question what had just happened. She exited the theater as quickly as she could and picked up her pace as she reached the college green. She had to talk to Malcolm.

*

When Malcolm opened his front door, Abby pushed past him into the house. She'd never been more nervous in her life. She turned abruptly. "I won't beat around the bush. I've had my suspicions, and Pat Wiggins confirmed them. You're a vampire."

"Pat's a good . . . woman." He stepped toward her—glided, actually. "Would you like to sit down?"

She zigzagged backward, and then leaned against the arm of a wing chair. "Whoa. I've suspected since that first night at your house." She eased herself into the chair, crossed her legs, and jiggled her foot. Her eyes roamed the room, taking in the Victorian couch and the ornately carved buffet—furnishings that screamed *time warp*. She pressed a hand to her heart and said, "I've done quite a bit of research on vampires, and all the pieces fit, except for the one about burning in sunlight." She rose slowly from the chair. "I don't hear you denying it."

He touched her cheek, leaving a frisson of electricity that made Abby jump. "I don't want to frighten you, Abby."

She glanced down at her trembling hands, and then up into his eyes. "Part of me wants to run."

"There's no need to run. I have amazing self-control, but then, you probably researched that, too." One side of his mouth turned up.

"Oh, yeah, I'm an expert." She rolled her eyes, and then took one step back. "Look, I need to get a few things straight."

"By all means."

"First, one more visit from Kyle's friends, and I'll have to get a whole new cast." She rubbed her arms.

"Ah, yes, now the pieces fit. Those goons belong to a coven of young vampires, and Kyle fits the profile of a vampire wannabe."

"Oh, God, that's insane," Abby said. "I've been working with Kyle for years. What could have possessed him?"

"I've seen it happen before with people who lack self-confidence and can't distinguish themselves any other way. They are easily led. They see vampires as all-powerful, and they'll do anything to become one."

Abby's jaw dropped, and then she said, "So, what do we do? We can't sit back and let Kyle and these vampires run rough-shod over us."

"Without evidence, I'm afraid our hands are tied. And even with evidence, the current vampire council is corrupt. As far as I know, they could be in collusion with the Night Fright boys. I've suspected that coven was responsible for the coed's death a couple of years ago. Maybe Kyle was involved."

Abby shook her head. "Kyle? Geez, that's crazy. He's always seemed so meek."

"More weak than meek. People like Kyle enjoy witnessing fear. They want to be part of manipulating chaos, of having the kind of power and attributes vampires possess."

"Speaking of chaos, I thought the cast was going to freak out when those guys vanished."

Malcolm smiled. "You did a lovely job of circumventing that situation, by the way."

"I had to think fast. Once I knew for sure you were a vampire, I started to worry about you exposing yourself, and then those guys showed up with their glowing eyes, and then they practically jetted out of the room, and . . . " Abby threw up her hands.

"You were worried about me?"

"Yes." Abby let herself look into Malcolm's eyes. "This has been your closely guarded secret. I'd be heartbroken if the play exposed you." Then, uncomfortable with her confession, she added, "Why did they leave when you asked them to?"

"Because I am an old vampire, and they have to obey me, at least until they have enough evidence."

"Evidence?"

"Clues that I might betray my identity. That would be cause for them to report me to the vampire council, who would inflict the true death."

"Why would they want to kill you? And—what's the true death?"

"Killing me wouldn't be their main goal. What they really want is to harness my ability to function in daylight."

"How could they do that?"

"It's in my blood. They'd drain me."

Abby shuddered. "And—what's the true death?"

"I'm already dead from a human standpoint, but dying as a vampire is obliteration to dust. I wouldn't have much choice in the matter if the council ruled against me."

"And by going to the Goth club . . . and rescuing me . . . you put yourself in danger?" Her heart raced. "Why would you do that for me?" She braced herself. What did she want his answer to be? That he was drawn to her? That he wanted her?

Malcolm walked to his fireplace. Abby watched him scanning the photographs on the mantel. He stopped at a portrait of a woman posed on a Victorian settee. "Honestly?" he asked, turning to her.

"Please." She longed for him to say something, anything that might indicate he cared.

"You set my heart in motion. That hasn't happened to me since I became a vampire, and as much as I've tried, I can't seem to ignore it."

Abby's heart pounded. "Why me?"

"You remind me of my wife. Your faces favor each other, and she had that same expression, like she was waiting for something wonderful to happen." He paused for a deep breath. "She was also brave, and you've got your own brand of pluck."

Abby laughed. "Pluck? Yeah, I've heard that before. You're sure you don't mean moxie?"

"No, I mean skill and perseverance." He ran his hand over the top of the mantel photograph. "She died during the war."

Abby didn't need to ask which war. "Tell me about her."

Still looking at the portrait of Sarah, Malcolm said, "She was extraordinarily kind. After I was called to war, she kept up the work on the farm. She labored with the farmhands, plowing the fields and tending the livestock." Malcolm shook his head. "She worked too hard, trying to take care of everything in my absence."

"So, when we went to Caroline Foster's house on the ghost tour, your wife was the Sarah who died in the house? And you were the Malcolm in the letter?"

Malcolm ran a hand through his hair and sighed. "Yes. Sarah went to her sister's after the battle to help. She nursed soldiers in town. Caroline tried to contact me when Sarah took ill with typhoid fever, but I was on a mission where I couldn't be reached. I could have saved her."

Abby's heart ached for him. "Oh, Malcolm, you don't know that."

"She was already weakened from the farm work when she went to her sister's. Not everyone dies of typhoid. If I'd been there to take care of her . . . "

"I'm so sorry." Abby touched Malcolm's arm. "You must have loved her very much."

Sarah was remarkable—such courage and selflessness. How could Abby measure up? And Malcolm was human when he loved Sarah. Could a vampire feel that depth of love?

Chapter Ten

Malcolm and Sarah moved out of Caroline's house and back to their home one week after Malcolm's injury. During that same week, Robert E. Lee retreated to Virginia with what was left of his battered army. The Confederates had been relatively kind to their property. They'd taken all the crops and left a receipt, not that Confederate money was worth anything in Pennsylvania, but it was a nice gesture.

More important to Malcolm, they hadn't burned or desecrated his land. And since Malcolm had ordered Sully to take the livestock to the old homestead east of town, he had his cows, pigs, and chickens back. His only problem was what to feed them.

As he and Sarah sat on their front porch after a hot summer day of plowing fields under and replanting, the dust of distant hooves clouded the horizon, and Malcolm stiffened, anticipating a harbinger. He rose from his chair and watched as Sarah gripped the arms of hers. When two blue-uniformed riders came into focus, Malcolm offered Sarah his hand and pulled her up to stand by him.

"I knew this was inevitable, but I'd hoped they'd let you spend a few more days at home," she said, squeezing his hand.

"We were lucky to have the time we did." He leaned over and kissed her.

The soldiers dismounted at the barn, tied up their mounts, and strode determinedly toward Malcolm. When they stopped at the steps to the porch, both soldiers saluted their superior officer, and then removed their hats. "Colonel," the shorter of the two said, "we have your orders." He retrieved an envelope from his breast pocket and handed it to Malcolm. The bars on their shoulders indicated their rank as lieutenant.

"Thank you, lieutenant . . . ?" Malcolm asked.

"I'm Jack Wright, sir," said the shorter man, "and this is Clayton Norcross. We're both West Point men, as I know you are, sir. We're cavalry, too, sir."

Malcolm smiled at them and nodded his approval. He turned the envelope in his hands, noting Sarah's glance at the fateful missive.

"Gentlemen," she said, "please have a seat." She swept an open palm to the porch chairs. "May I offer you a glass of lemonade?"

"That would be nice, Mrs. McClellan." Lieutenant Norcross, who sported a bushy mustache, ambled toward a chair. His spurs clicked on the wood planks as Sarah departed for the kitchen.

Malcolm inquired about army movements and new appointments but waited until Sarah returned before breaking the wax seal on the envelope. He flicked the page of parchment open and held it in both hands.

"Colonel McClellan," he began, "I commend you and your Pennsylvania regiment for exceptional valor in the three days of Gettysburg, and I trust you are recovered from your wounds. Because of my special confidence in your patriotism and integrity, I hereby authorize and empower you to raise a company of picked men and proceed to Virginia to intercept the movement of Confederate troops and supplies via railway. You are requested to act with secrecy and discretion. Communication will be restricted. Sincerely, General George Gordon Meade, commander, Army of the Potomac."

Malcolm folded the letter and returned it to its envelope.

"When he asks you to handpick men, just where exactly does he suppose you're going to find them?" Sarah crossed her arms. "Don't you need special skills for railroad work?"

"We're not *building* railroads, Sarah," Malcolm said. "Most of our work will be in destroying railway ties."

"And what does he mean by 'restricted communication?' You won't be able to get help if you need it?"

"I'm sure we could get reinforcements if the conditions were dire, but I think it's more a matter of being out of touch with home. Once we get moving, no one will know where we are."

Sarah's brow knitted and she chewed on her bottom lip. And then she slapped her skirt. "Well, gentlemen, I'm not one to sit back and let luck determine destiny. Might I suggest you join my husband on this venture?" Sarah asked the two lieutenants. "You both seem able-bodied and intelligent, and it would ease my mind some to know he'd have experienced cavalry officers at his side."

"I believe I can speak for Lieutenant Norcross in saying that we'd both be honored, ma'am, that is, if the colonel will have us." Lieutenant Wright nodded toward Malcolm.

"I'd be the one honored, lieutenant. Report back to me day after tomorrow. By then, I should be able to roust a few more men for the job." Malcolm chuckled. "In fact, there are several from my regiment who would enjoy nothing more than overtaking a train by horseback."

"I don't know, sir, some of these new steam engines can be pretty fast," Lieutenant Norcross said. "I've even heard that there's one that's haunted."

"Yes, I've heard those rumors, too," Malcolm said.

"A haunted train?" Sarah laughed. "That's poppycock."

Malcolm hadn't bothered Sarah with the rumors, and as he regarded her now, this woman who put no stock in the supernatural, he wished he felt as confident as she did about the nonexistence of ghosts. He'd felt their eerie presence on the battlefield, seen their wispy shapes sway above the bodies of fallen soldiers. He couldn't dismiss the possibility of a haunted train.

*

When the soldiers took their leave, Malcolm and Sarah watched them mount their horses and disappear over the ridge, leaving the same cloud of dust that had heralded their arrival.

"Funny how life can change in the matter of an hour," Sarah said. "Perhaps 'funny' is the wrong word—more like heartbreaking."

She leaned into Malcolm, and he wrapped an arm around her. "Since I cannot *send* letters, I shall write them anyway—and save them for your return."

"I will return, Sarah. I may not be able to receive your letters on this mission, but I shall savor them when I get home." Malcolm turned up her chin and kissed her mouth. "Since I met you, my reckless abandon ceased. Nothing is more important to me than living my life with you by my side."

"Just how reckless were you?" Sarah traced a finger down the hollow of Malcolm's neck and across his collarbone.

"Let's just say that I thought I was invincible, but I suppose many young men do until they have something to live for."

"All I ask is for you to come back to me. It's all I'll ever ask."

Chapter Eleven

Now that Abby knew Malcolm's true identity, he wanted to show her that a vampire was still a man; that even though he was a monster, he could be genteel with a woman.

He wanted to court her, but how did men court women in the twenty-first century? In the nineteenth century, a man had to request the pleasure of spending time with a woman through her father, and if there was a match to be made, it was based more on family standing and land acquisition than attraction.

My, how times had changed. Where did one take a woman on a date? Malcolm had seen a few movies. He supposed that was an option. But he wanted to do something more physical with Abby, something that would bring color to her cheeks and leave her breathless. Making love to her would accomplish that, but he couldn't take that chance. What if he got lost in the moment and bit her? Restraining himself would be extremely difficult.

What would be safe?

Aha. Perhaps she likes horses.

*

When her cell phone chirped, Abby didn't recognize the number on her caller I.D.

"Hello, this is Abby Potter," she said, anticipating a student.

"Good morning, Abby. This is Malcolm." He cleared his throat.

"Oh, hi." Her heart sped up. "What're you up to this fine Saturday morning?"

"I was going to take Midnight for a ride. Do you ride . . . horses?"

"For a moment I was picturing you putting your horse in a

car." She laughed. "Yes, I ride."

"I have a lovely mare, Matilda, not too spirited. She hasn't been ridden for a while, but if you're at all adept, she's easy to handle."

"I grew up on a farm in Virginia. I guess you didn't know that."

"I know very little about you, Abby, but I'd like to learn."

Abby wanted to pinch herself. Did he really want to get to know her? Heat rose in her cheeks. "Here's my life in a nutshell. I'm an only child. My parents are both doctors. They married late in life, so they wasted no time having me."

"Are they still living?"

"Yes, they're retired now. They do a lot of volunteer work."

"That doesn't surprise me. You have a caring nature." He paused. "So, would you like to go riding with me?"

"Yes."

*

Abby knocked on Malcolm's front door, her heart in her throat. She wore jeans, a turtleneck, a sweater, and a windbreaker. The snow had recently melted, and with a clear sky and no wind, the ride wouldn't be too cold. She took a deep breath, inhaling the crisp, cool air and attempting to calm her jitters. She half expected Malcolm to answer the door in Civil War garb.

When the door swung open, he was dressed almost identically to her. She laughed. "I was getting ready to salute."

"Wait until Midnight sees me. He doesn't think I'm serious if I'm not in uniform." He swept his arm aside for Abby to enter. "He's descended from my Civil War stallion, also Midnight."

"How often do you do your Civil War thing?"

"I travel to a lot of battle sites for annual re-enactments, and the schedule is even busier now that we're celebrating the sesquicentennial. I always do Gettysburg in July, and before that, I'm planning to take Midnight to Shiloh in late March. I may do Chancellorsville in June."

"How does it make you feel, reliving the war?"

Malcolm had been walking through the parlor ahead of Abby, but he stopped and turned. "No one has ever asked me that. No one has known I was there." He sighed. "It makes me feel almost human to return to the time I was mortal." A smile turned up the corners of his mouth. "And you make me feel human."

*

Matilda's chestnut coat shone in the sunlight, and the white blaze down her nose highlighted her soulful eyes. Abby grew up riding, and she took to Matilda immediately.

"Are Matilda and Midnight lovers?" Abby patted Matilda's neck while Malcolm saddled her up.

"They're more than that. They're right married, as we would have said in the 1860s." Malcolm scratched the mare's flank. "She's had two foals, but the second one almost killed her, so Midnight is now a gelding."

Midnight's tail twitched.

"Poor fellow. Guess that was the end of his fun," Abby said.

"I think he's just as happy to have his sugar cubes and apples." Malcolm laughed. "And he's definitely more even-tempered."

Malcolm helped Abby mount, lifting her by the waist as though she weighed ten pounds. She didn't want him to let go. He handed her the reins. "She's sensitive. You shouldn't have to give her more than a small tug in any direction. Squeeze with your legs if you want her to speed up."

Abby wondered if that same move worked on Malcolm.

Once they had the horses out of the barn, Malcolm mounted Midnight. "Are you comfortable with a gallop?" he asked.

"Sure, as long as Matilda knows where she's going."

"She'd follow Midnight to the ends of the earth."

As they headed into the cool November air, Abby thought the

same of herself. She'd follow Malcolm anywhere, but after more than a century of living in the shadows, would this play . . . and she . . . unravel the safety net he'd so carefully built for himself? Would she be his undoing? He seemed completely human today, but he had an alternate nature that could surface at any time. She'd experienced it on the ghost tour when he made that remark about biting her neck.

Watching Malcolm ahead of her, his broad shoulders against the wind, the most sensible move would be to turn from him and never look back.

Chapter Twelve

Another goodbye. Sarah squeezed her eyes shut as she clung to Malcolm, memorizing the feel of his arms around her, longing for a life in which the longest goodbye would be a trip to the market. With her face pressed against his chest, she inhaled the clean scent of his new wool uniform and prayed it would return without bloodstains or bullet holes.

"What is it, darling?" Malcolm's clean-shaven chin rubbed against Sarah's head, catching tendrils of her hair.

"Nothing, it's nothing," she said, pulling him closer.

"No, I know you. I felt the shudder through your body. Tell me what you were thinking."

She pushed away, looked up, and squinted. "I was trying to remember a time when the only thing we worried about was how much the pigs would bring at market."

He brought her back to his chest. "You're dreaming. We were never together—without war."

She sighed. "Yes, you're right, but it was a lovely dream."

"Don't stop dreaming, Sarah." He kissed the top of her head.

"I won't. I shall dream of you every night—until you return."

*

Malcolm, Clayton, Jack, and Malcolm's two men from his regiment, William and Henry, rode out of Gettysburg on August 7, a hot and dusty day. Sarah waved from the porch until Malcolm disappeared from sight, melding with the horizon as the black speck of his stallion dissolved to an ink dot against the blue sky. Her heart sank in her chest when he disappeared, and she leaped down the steps and ran toward the western sky, lifting her skirts and pumping her legs to reach the ridge and catch another glimpse. Alas, nothing but horizon. She collapsed in a heap onto the dry ground, clutching handfuls of dirt, and then rolled to her back. She squinted into the sun and whispered, "Come back to me."

*

After two days of near constant riding, the men set up camp on the Virginia-Maryland border in dense woods within sight of the railway line. Malcolm sent William and Henry to scout for Confederate camps, and Clayton headed east to report their position to General Meade. Their strategy was to first get a handle on the schedule of the trains, and then to destroy the railway ties, derailing the trains.

The Confederates had used trains effectively to move troops over the past several years, and in fact, their victory at Chancellorsville was largely due to reinforcements who arrived by rail. But the tenor of the war had changed. Everyone felt it, from the teenage private to the seasoned general. Lee's attempt to invade the North had failed. He was on the run.

"Where do you suppose General Lee is, colonel?" Jack poked at the dwindling fire that had warmed their dinner of beans and hardtack made palatable by Sarah's preserves.

"I'd wager he's heading to shore up Richmond." Malcolm swiped at the crumbs on his chin, smiling to himself. At home, Sarah would have wiped his chin, clicking her tongue as she let her hand linger on his cheek.

"So, if they're not heading in this direction, that'd mean we won't see many troops on the trains."

"I would agree." Malcolm strode to where Midnight was tethered to a tree. He offered the horse a carrot.

"Well, pardon my ignorance, colonel, but then why in heck are we here?"

Malcolm gazed into the clear night sky, blanketed with stars. An owl's mournful cry pierced the calm. "I believe we're here to squelch rumors, lieutenant."

"Sorry, sir, but I'm not following."

"There's been talk of a haunted train—inhabited by ghosts."

Jack rolled on his back and clutched his knees to his chest. His subsequent guffaw made Midnight start, and Malcolm patted the big horse's nose to calm him. When Jack returned to a cross-legged position, he said, "I've had some strange assignments over the last couple years, but this has to be the strangest." He scratched his head. "You don't really believe this talk of ghosts, do you, colonel?"

"I don't know what to believe," Malcolm said as he ran a hand over two days of beard stubble, "but I'm itching to find out."

Chapter Thirteen

Night Fright was becoming Kyle's second home. As he pulled into the club's parking lot, taking the spot next to Arlo's black truck, his chest swelled with pride. Soon, he'd be immortal.

Arlo nodded him through the club to a back room where Kyle plunked down on a white vinyl sofa that provided little give under his slight weight. With an upturned palm, he deferred to Arlo.

"We've overlooked a valuable resource," Arlo said.

Kyle waited. If he played a guessing game with Arlo, he'd likely get smacked upside the head.

Arlo grinned. "Malcolm's got a thing for Abby. Otherwise, he would never have agreed to this play. He's been slippery as an eel for years, and now that we've almost got him, I'm getting impatient." He perched on the corner of his desk, crossing his legs yoga-style. "I don't want him to settle into a groove. He needs some incentive to bring out his true nature, and that's where you come in."

"Sorry, I'm not following." Kyle clamped his hand over his mouth. He shouldn't have interrupted Arlo.

Sneering at Kyle, Arlo continued. "Vampires are exceedingly jealous. If you make a move on Abby, Malcolm will react. He won't be able to help himself. He's tuned to her."

"So, what do I do, kiss her in front of him?"

"No, just get her alone and make an overture. He'll be able to sense it. He'll appear."

"Am I taking my life in my hands?" Kyle chuckled nervously.

"Nah, he won't do anything overt, but it'll get his juices pumping, and the more we can force him to feel his true nature, the more likely he'll be to let his guard down in the play."

"I've never come on to Abby," Kyle said. "She'll think it's a joke."

"It doesn't matter what she thinks. Malcolm will buy it." Arlo unfolded from his pretzel pose and landed on the floor without a sound.

Kyle grinned. He'd be that graceful . . . soon.

"She may be surprised by your come-on, but so what? She's collateral damage. We won't let her live once we have Malcolm."

*

In spite of her niggling fears about Malcolm's safety, Abby couldn't stay away from him. Whether it was his vampire magnetism or his humanity that lured her, her sexual frustration was mounting exponentially. Tonight she was going to take charge of the situation.

She chose a hot pink cashmere sweater with a plunging V neckline. She would typically pair it with a sleeveless turtleneck, but tonight she layered it with a lacy camisole that allowed more than a hint of cleavage. Push-up bra. Thong. The long sweater hugged her butt, and she wore black tights to emphasize her long legs. Ankle-high boots with three-inch heels completed the ensemble. She pulled her hair back in a ponytail and secured it with a jeweled barrette. And she hoped to get her money's worth out of the bikini wax . . . her first one *ever* . . . that she'd endured that afternoon. She spritzed herself with J'Adore by Christian Dior. *Hey, if it's good enough for Charlize Theron . . .*

Arriving at Malcolm's at seven p.m., she turned off her car's engine and took a few deep breaths. She pulled down her visor mirror and batted her eyelashes. That new lash-lengthening mascara was a wonder.

Malcolm, in a heather gray sweater and charcoal gray slacks, met her at the door. His sweater sleeves were pushed up to his elbows (such gorgeous forearms), and he was barefoot. Abby supposed his feet didn't get cold, or maybe they were always cold, and it didn't bother him.

He smiled. "Incredible." He looked her up and down. "You look . . . and smell . . . amazing."

She decided to dive in while the night was young. "Are you ever planning to make a pass at me?"

His eyebrows shot up. "I've certainly thought about it."

"How *often* have you thought about it?"

"Would every minute of every day suffice?"

"What's stopping you?" She crossed her arms under her breasts and pushed them up into the deep V of her sweater.

"This is uncharted territory for me, Abby. I've never had a relationship—as a vampire."

She touched his elbow, and then ran her hand up his arm, feeling his muscles tense beneath her fingers. "It can't be that different. Making love is the same, right?"

"Yes—and no. Sex is the same, but I have a strong desire, overwhelming really, to taste your blood. It will take every ounce of my control to keep from biting you. I'd say that's a major departure from what most people would consider a 'normal' relationship. And I have the ability to coerce you, but I won't. This has to be a conscious decision for you."

"You're an honorable man, Malcolm. I trust you." *Honorable.* Such an old-fashioned word, but it suited him.

"As much as I want you, it won't be easy to restrain my instincts."

"I'm ready to take that chance." She pressed a hand to her heart. "I won't pretend I'm not frightened. I've never walked on the wild side."

"Wild isn't what I had in mind. We'll start slow."

Her pulse raced like a hummingbird's. She was taking a chance, probably the biggest chance of her life, but need overcame reason. "I'm in."

"Are you absolutely sure?"

Abby nodded. The desire to be in his arms eclipsed her fear. She leaned into him, feeling the weight of his big body. He wrapped her in his arms, and everything else melted away. She tilted her chin, and he lowered his head. They kissed. He tasted fantastic, like her favorite smoky shiraz, but better. His thumb caressed the tender spot below her ear while his other hand cupped her head. Her tongue sought his, and he responded with longing and finesse, not too forceful, but not soft, either. It was the best kiss of her life, fraught with intention, and she trusted where he was going with it. The man she'd admired for years wanted her, and oh, she wanted him. Her toes curled.

When the perfect kiss ended, he held her shoulders and gazed at her with a final question in his eyes. She nodded yes, unable to speak. This was what she wanted. He ran his knuckles down her cheek, and then he walked to the mantel, lit a candle and handed the candlestick to her. "The bedroom's upstairs, second door on the right. I'll be up in a few minutes."

The stairs creaked as Abby ascended. When she reached the top step, the reality of what she was about to do made her grab the banister. She looked down at Malcolm. "I'm not on birth control."

"I thought you'd done your vampire research." He smiled. "We can't reproduce, and we can't acquire or transmit disease."

"Okay, then. We're good." *Holy moley, this is really happening.*

Entering the room Malcolm indicated, her eyes scanned the antique furnishings. She set the candlestick on the dresser. A four-poster bed with an heirloom quilt anchored the room. Next to it stood a washstand with a bowl and pitcher. Under the lace-curtained window, a little vanity languished. A length of fabric lay folded on the vanity stool. Abby felt drawn to pick up the fabric, and it unfurled to reveal a lovely nightgown. It was a sheer shift, floor length with its only adornment a row of crocheted flowers at the deeply scooped neckline. Shaking it gently to dispel wrinkles, the gown released the heavenly scent of lavender, and the fabric swirled like it had been set free. Something compelled her to put it on. Laying it on the bed, she peeled off her clothes, and then slipped on the cream-colored gown.

Her whole body tingled. She stood barefoot, gazing in the vanity mirror, when hands caressed her shoulders. She hadn't heard Malcolm enter the room, and hers was the only reflection in the mirror.

Her heart raced as she verified two more vampire characteristics; a soundless approach and no reflection. A tug loosened her ponytail from the barrette, and strong fingers massaged her temples and then snaked their way through her hair, cascading it around her shoulders.

"You're beautiful," he whispered in her ear. "Seeing you in that gown—you can't know what that does to me."

She turned and looked up at him, inhaling his heady scent of spice and cloves. She ran her hands down his powerful chest. When his muscles tensed, the shock waves rippled through her body. She opened her lips to welcome his velvet tongue, and the world stopped spinning on its axis.

*

Malcolm wrenched his lips from Abby's. With lightning speed and pent-up desire, he threw off his sweater, and then he remembered his promise to start slow. He ached to ravish her, but more than that, he needed to savor what they'd both longed for. He touched her mouth, her face, her hair, gently caressing and exploring. He pressed his forehead to hers and took a deep breath. Then he slowly unzipped his pants and let them drop. No boxers or briefs to remove.

He'd become accustomed to a constant erection in Abby's presence, and now standing naked, knowing she would finally be his, an explosion of suppressed lust made his fangs extend. Retracting them took every ounce of his willpower.

He eased the gown over her head, and then swept the quilt off the bed. He picked her up and placed her on the antique bed. His cock brushed her naked hip as he stood next to her, and he closed his eyes as her hand caressed him. He reclined next to her on the cool bed linens, tracing the outline of her jaw with his fingers and continuing down her arm and hip, committing her body to memory. She was so beautiful. He brushed his fingers across her nipples, which immediately hardened at his touch.

He pulled her on top of him and stroked her back, pressing her breasts into his chest, heart-to-heart. He moved his hands down to her buttocks, spreading his fingers wide and cupping her there. Moving her hips in sensuous circles against his cock, he nibbled on her bottom lip.

She moaned, and then she reached down and embraced his shaft. He caught her wrists, trying to hold back, but her grip was firm and insistent. Her words came in a breathless rasp. "I need you inside me *now*."

He slid full into her and lay motionless for a moment, letting her adapt to the length and breadth of him. He tilted her hips, encouraging her to sit up. Bending her knees tight against his hips, she straddled him, arching her back so that her nipples, flushed dark, jutted toward him as she thrust her head back. The light from the full moon outside his bedroom window cast a shadow of their entwined forms on the wall, and an owl signaled their coupling with a triumphant hoot.

Malcolm moved his hands to Abby's thighs and opened her folds like a flower, circling her sensitive bud and capturing it between his thumbs.

She ran her hands up and down his body. Her eyes rolled back, and Malcolm knew she was close to the throes of her release. He could bite her now. Oh, God, he wanted to bite her. He could almost taste her sweet blood, and if he punctured her artery as she climaxed, she'd allow him to drink from her. He could feel that she would. *But no, stop this madness, Malcolm. She trusts you. She honors you.* He had to maintain control.

Shaking off his dark thoughts, he lifted her off his cock and moved her alongside him on the bed, her back to his chest. He ran his hand down the smooth porcelain of her back, and then lifted her leg high in the air. He positioned himself slowly, and then penetrated her sheath from behind. She took his cue and grasped her knee so that she was splayed wide, and he cupped her mound, his fingers dancing across her wet bud, which he pleasured to the point of no return. He felt her climax begin to pulse before she gave into it, and when she did, her entire body jerked with the spasms of her delight, which sent him over the edge. He exploded into her, riding the wave of his release until it finally subsided, and they collapsed together. Malcolm wrapped his arms tightly around her and breathed into her hair. "Abby."

He'd never thought he could care so deeply for another woman. Had he truly turned a corner by bringing Abby into his life? What would Sarah think?

Chapter Fourteen

Inadequate. Frivolous. Abby couldn't shake the self-doubt. She'd asked Malcolm to tell her about Sarah, and she knew it was good for him to be able to talk about the woman he'd loved and lost, but she hadn't considered the fallout effect it would have on her own self-image.

She had never been the kind of woman to compare herself to others, but next to Sarah, trait-for-trait, she felt woefully lacking. Her life had been a cakewalk; Sarah's had been a marathon of hardship. While Malcolm was at war, Sarah had waged her own battles on the farm, maintaining crops and livestock with only two farmhands. In the aftermath of the Battle of Gettysburg, Sarah had tirelessly nursed wounded soldiers in a makeshift hospital.

Abby ticked off the times she'd met with true adversity. There was the summer of 2000, when she and three other Girl Scouts had gotten lost in the Blue Ridge Mountains. She'd kept the group's spirits up with songs and games. True, she didn't succumb to the hysterics of the other girls, but that was just her practical nature. Then in college, she'd blown the whistle on a farm in rural Pennsylvania where horses were dying from neglect. *The Gettysburg Times* had written a story about her. So, she'd done things to earn merit badges and accolades, but had she ever put herself in harm's way for someone else?

Malcolm deserved someone with true courage.

*

"Drink your orange juice, Abby. Mortals need vitamin C to ward off colds, and there's a definite chill in the air today." Malcolm pushed the glass of juice across the kitchen table to Abby. He could

81

tell she was brooding by the way her eyebrows knit together. And she looked so vulnerable . . . and adorable. How had he resisted her for so long? "Why don't you tell me what's wrong."

"Sarah was resilient. I've never faced real adversity. It makes me feel . . . unsuitable for you." She shifted in her chair.

"You are far from unsuitable." He wished he could convince her. God, she had no reason to feel insecure.

"But you and Sarah had so much in common." She frowned.

"Because we were farmers?"

"No. I'm serious. You were in sync."

"Not entirely. We had our quarrels, but it was a different time, Abby. Women were dependent on men. They rarely bucked the system. Like most of the women during the Civil War, Sarah did what she had to do in the face of adversity. I'm not saying that to diminish her bravery, because she was courageous, but you've never met with that kind of conflict. I have no doubt you'd rise to the occasion."

"You're giving me too much credit."

He wished she could believe him. If only there was a way to convince her.

*

The following afternoon, Abby sat at her office desk, gnawing on the gooey center of her fourth candy sucker of the day. She typically allowed herself three, but today her musings about Sarah had required additional thought, aided by chewing.

She'd long suspected that the ten ghost tours in Gettysburg had a kernel of truth in their tales, but she only half believed. Now that Malcolm was in her life, she knew there was a paranormal world out there that really existed. And then there was Pat, who had her own supernatural thing going. With Pat's guidance, Abby had done some research on conjuring ghosts. She learned that spirits could be summoned by holding an object that had belonged to the deceased.

When she'd worn Sarah's gown, her whole body tingled when the fabric touched her skin. Today, she brought the gown to her office, carefully wrapped in tissue and transported in a box that now sat on her desk.

As she chewed on her candy stick, she stared at the box. She'd planned to take the gown home and attempt her summoning there, but curiosity and impatience got the best of her. She had no appointments, twenty minutes before her next class, and with her office tucked away at the end of the hall, complete privacy. Inhaling and then exhaling to the count of four, she chucked the stick in her wastebasket. She took hand sanitizer from her purse, squirted it into her palm and rubbed vigorously. Wiping her hands on a paper towel, she removed the gown from its box and placed it on her legs. As she fingered the fabric, the sweet scent of lavender danced around her head. Her pulse quickened.

She pushed away from her desk, got up from her chair and held the gown at arm's length. Malcolm had told her that she resembled Sarah, though Abby was a bit taller and her hair was a shade lighter. Abby adjusted the gown in front of her to where she thought it would have rested on Sarah's shoulders. She imagined Sarah's light brown hair grazing the embroidered flowers on the scooped collar, and she could almost see Sarah's fingers touching the silky leaves so lovingly crafted by her sister, Caroline.

"I fear I can't measure up to you, Sarah." Abby said to the gown, and then closed her eyes. A cool breeze drifted across her eyelids. She steeled herself.

"I wasn't special, Abby." The words echoed softly against the walls of Abby's small office.

Abby almost fainted. She thought the gown had power, but she hadn't considered how she'd react if her suspicion proved true. She gulped. "Tell me what to do." Abby let go of the gown as she sensed a presence suspending it. She opened her eyes. There before her stood Sarah, translucent like an angel and surrounded by an aura of yellow-white light. Her presence was dynamic. Waves of energy spun wisps of hair around her face and billowed the gown around her small frame.

"You can make him whole again." Sarah raised a hand. Her cool fingers brushed across Abby's cheek like butterfly kisses. "There are many times I could have appeared to Malcolm over the years, and I chose not to. I knew that if I interfered in his life, he would never move on."

"He loved you so much, Sarah."

"And I adored him." Sarah smiled. "But our time is history, and he needs to let go. If not, his guilt will destroy him. You are his future. You must save him from himself."

"Will I see you again?" Abby wanted to gather Sarah in her arms to thank her.

"No, you have your life. I am content. Do not tell Malcolm we met." Sarah put a finger to her lips. "Simply love him." The light that surrounded Sarah became more intense, almost blinding. Abby blinked hard, and then the gown fell to the floor. She reached behind her for the arms of the chair and slumped back into it, pressing a hand to her racing heart.

She didn't have much time to still her heart or collect her thoughts because the door to her office flew open and there stood Pamela Shields, impatiently tapping a needle-nosed boot in Abby's direction.

"There you are," Pamela said. "I've been looking all over campus for you."

"Well, this *is* my office. You could have started here." Abby almost rolled her eyes but caught herself just in time. It was too easy to be sarcastic with Pamela. "What can I do you for?"

Pamela ran a finger across the length of Abby's desk.

Trying it on for size?

"Oh, I just thought we could have a chat. I've been curious about a few things."

Keeping her expression neutral was getting painful. Like she and Pamela could chat. The last time they'd tried to have a civil discussion, it soon escalated to a shouting match, and Pamela's shrieking could shatter glass. "A chat? Seriously?"

"Yeah." Pamela checked her finger for dust, blew on it, and then pointed it at Abby. "I was in Philly the other night with some friends, and we thought we'd slum it at a Goth club. Turns out there were a few guys there who said they recognized me from Gettysburg College. They were those weirdos who were sitting in the back of the theater last week. Pretty cute weirdos, actually, except for the wall-eyed one. I thought it was strange they would have recognized me. I was just sitting in the audience, but they must have looked my way when I screamed. Still, it was odd they remembered me."

Because they're vampires, you idiot. They see everything. Abby struggled to keep herself in check. "Don't sell yourself short, Pamela. You're a beautiful woman. Of course they'd notice you." Abby almost gagged, but plastered on a smile instead.

Pamela narrowed her eyes. "No, it was more than that. I think they're on some serious drugs. Their eyes were bloodshot. And get this, they wanted the skinny on Dr. McClellan. The way he'd told them to leave the theater, I knew something was up. These guys asked me a bunch of questions about him, like if he mingled with humans. Yeah, that's what they said, 'mingled with humans.' As opposed to what, zombies?" Pamela harrumphed. "They also wanted to know whether I'd ever seen him do anything out of the ordinary, like roam the campus in the dead of night."

"I guess they thought *you* roam the campus at night. They must have taken *you* for a zombie." Abby chuckled.

"You think that's funny?" Pamela raised a perfectly plucked eyebrow. "I think there's something very strange going on here. Remember that coed who was murdered a few years ago? I'll bet Dr. McClellan had something to do with it."

Abby balled her fists under her desk. She wanted to smack Pamela across her Cupid 's bow lips. "Dr. McClellan is one of the most respected professors at this school. I'd stop spreading unfounded rumors if I were you."

Pamela sucked in her cheeks and nodded her head. "That's what I thought you'd say. And you know what, I'm glad you defended him, because that tells me that you two have something going."

"You mean we planned the girl's murder together?" Abby threw up her hands. "Pamela, you missed your calling. You really should have been a private investigator. You've just taken deductive reasoning to a new low. Let's call the police." Abby picked up her desk phone and offered it to Pamela. "I can't tell you how much I appreciate your coming here today because I've needed to get this off my chest. Confession is good for the soul."

Pamela waved the phone away. "You always were good at twisting words. I'm not saying you collaborated in a murder, but there is something going on between the two of you. And there's much more to Dr. McClellan than meets the eye." She licked her lips. "Although what meets the eye is really hot."

Abby stood up from her desk and walked to her office door. She leaned against it and crossed her arms. "I've heard enough of your nonsense for one day, *Miss* Shields. It's a shame that someone with your talent has to stoop so low. If you had any integrity, you could be successful. Instead, you resort to scare tactics and innuendo. Couldn't hack it in New York, could you? Now you're back here stirring up trouble. What exactly do you want? My job? Come on—out with it!"

"Oh, I do want your job, and I'll get it. But I'm also going to get to the bottom of whatever your vampire hero is up to."

Abby's heart stopped, until she remembered that Pamela was referring to Malcolm's role in the play, not him. She tried to breathe evenly. "Get out." She opened the door wide to allow Pamela's passage.

Pamela shrugged, adjusted the designer bag on her shoulder, and took one step toward the door. That's when she saw Sarah's gown on the floor. "What's this?" She bent toward the gown and reached out a hand.

Abby leaped to snatch up the gown, but Pamela was too quick. As soon as Pamela's hand touched the fabric, she shrieked and jumped back. "That thing shocked me!"

Abby bent to the gown and picked it up gently. "It's just static." She folded the gown and carefully placed it back in the box, covering it with tissue. "This is a valuable heirloom. I'm planning to make a replica for the costume department. It's for the play." She put it on her desk.

"For the play, eh?" Pamela smirked and wrapped her expensive scarf a bit tighter around her neck. "Interesting that it didn't shock *you*."

Abby wanted to strangle her—death by Hermes.

"All right," Pamela said with a sigh. "I'll leave you to your antiquities, but you haven't heard the last from me." She clip-clopped out of Abby's office, not bothering to shut the door.

Staring at the empty doorway for a moment, Abby took a few deep breaths and then checked her watch. *Shit!* She had five minutes to get across campus to her class, and she was never late. She liked to get there early so that if any of her students had questions, they'd have the opportunity to ask before class began. She grabbed her coat and flew out the door. She didn't lock it. She never did.

When she returned to her office after class, she immediately knew something was amiss. The box with Sarah's gown wasn't on her desk. She frantically searched every corner. The gown was gone. *Damn and double damn.* It didn't take long to figure out what had happened. Pamela had come back and taken it.

She'd made a promise to Sarah. Could she tell Malcolm the gown was missing without revealing that Sarah had appeared to her? She'd have to.

But first, she needed to visit Pat.

She wasted no time getting to Retro Mania. Pat was waiting for her at the front door, her arms crossed over her considerable bosom.

"Thought you'd never get here." Pat pulled Abby inside and flipped the closed sign on her front door. "You've got a real problem."

"I don't suppose you'll tell me what you know," Abby said, "or *how* you know it."

"Look, sweetie, there are some things best left unexplained. You're dealing with enough paranormal activity as it is. Someday, I'll clue you into mine, but for now, let's shed some light on your problem." She took Abby's hand and led her through a velvet curtain at the back of the shop. Abby had never been in the bowels of Pat's store, but she knew it was where her friend conducted fortune readings and séances.

Pat motioned for Abby to sit at a round table in the middle of the room. A large crystal ball in the center swirled with smoky activity.

"This could be a movie set." Abby scanned the walls, covered in shiny red wallpaper flocked with velvety fleur-de-lis. "Can you say 'stereotype?'" Abby suppressed a chuckle.

"Don't laugh. My clients expect the full monty, and I'm not one to disappoint. I could do what I do anywhere, as long as I have my crystal ball, but it's more believable with trappings."

With no windows in the room, Abby blinked to adjust her eyes to the dark. "So, this is where you conjure spirits?"

"Yeah, this is my playground, but we're not inviting anyone to participate today." She nodded to the crystal ball. "That's my portal. I've talked with Sarah."

Abby gripped the edges of the table. "I've talked with Sarah, too."

"I know. Do you have any idea how special that is—for a ghost to communicate directly with a human?"

"No, I don't know much about the spirit world, but Sarah was wonderful."

Pat winked at Abby. "I'll let you in on a little secret. I've been talking with her for years."

"Okay, Pat. It's time to 'fess up. What, exactly, are you?"

She shrugged. "I'm just your basic witch, with some gypsy thrown in for philosophy." She placed her hands on the crystal ball, sparks flew, and the room lit up with a candlelight glow.

Susan Blexrud

Abby scooted back in her chair and sat tall.

"That was just theatrics," Pat said, and then laughed. "We'll dispense with that." She removed her hands from the ball, but the glow in the room remained. "Here's what I think is going on." Pat leaned forward. "Sarah's glad that Pamela took the gown." She closed her eyes briefly, nodded, and then continued. "See, Malcolm's always felt guilty about Sarah's death, and she wants him to move past his guilt. She thinks if he can rescue the gown, he'll feel at least somewhat absolved."

"She truly was an amazing woman." She shook her head. "But Malcolm doesn't even know the gown's been taken . . . yet."

"Yeah, but you're going to tell him."

Abby's heart hiccupped. "I will . . . tonight." This was not a conversation she looked forward to.

*

Abby slid across Malcolm's living room floor in her stocking feet, emulating his glide while waiting for his return from a late class. She jumped when the click of the front door heralded his homecoming.

"Stressful day?" He approached her and touched her cheek.

"Pamela took Sarah's gown," Abby said quickly, before she lost her nerve. She turned her face away from Malcolm's touch, unable to face him. Her cheeks burned with her confession.

"What?"

"Pamela came to see me today, and she noticed the gown on my desk. I told her it was an heirloom, and that I was going to try to replicate it for the play. I guess she thought it was valuable."

"It is valuable . . . to me." Malcolm took Abby's chin and stared intently at her.

"Oh, God, I know that. I'm so sorry." Tears welled in her eyes, and her heart lurched.

Malcolm took a handkerchief from his pocket and dabbed her eyes. He bent his head and looked at her through his eyelashes. "And why did you need to replicate the gown?"

"I didn't really." She sighed. "I took the gown to my office because it inspires me, and I can feel Sarah's presence through it." *Did I say too much?*

Malcolm ran a hand through his hair. "Abby, this obsession with Sarah needs to stop."

"I didn't think it was an obsession . . . exactly."

"You have to stop comparing yourself to her." He took Abby's hand and pulled her to the wing chair. He pushed her gently down to sit, and then he knelt in front of her, between her knees. He placed his hands on her thighs. "I'm going to say this once, so listen to me carefully. I've lived a few generations longer than you, and I've had a lot of time to mull things over. I've witnessed the abolition of slavery and women getting the vote. I read *The Feminine Mystique* when it was in galleys." He grinned. "I used to be a chauvinist. The man Sarah fell in love with is not the man I am today. And as for Sarah, though I loved her deeply, she wasn't as independent as you are."

He squeezed her thighs, and desire engulfed her. She was ready to chuck the talk and make love right there on the floor, but she had to finish this thread. "How can you say that? She was so strong."

"She was certainly brave. She didn't run from adversity, but you are more proactive." He moved his hands up her thighs and massaged her crotch with his thumbs. "You create your own cyclones."

Abby moaned at his touch. She was putty in his hands. "Before we ravish each other, I have a couple of things I need to say. One, what should we do about the gown? And two, I've come to the conclusion that I'm the right woman for you."

Malcolm smiled. "In that order? All right. First, don't worry about the gown. I'll get it back. And second, I'm glad you've finally come to your senses." Malcolm moved his hands to the top of her tights, pulled them down her hips, off her feet, and threw them behind him. He unzipped his pants, unleashed his manhood, and pulled her hips to the edge of the chair. Pushing the thin strip of her panties aside, he eased his fingers into her dampness.

She gasped as he bent one of her knees up and rammed into her. He thrust deep, and then deeper, clutching her buttocks. She surrendered to his timing, closing her eyes in ecstasy and riding the wave until they collapsed together.

Chapter Fifteen

Several evenings later, Abby sat in Malcolm's kitchen, studying his statue-like presence across the table from her. She supposed it was his vampire ability to be so still, but she sensed he was silently reminiscing. "You've shared a lot about your life with Sarah, but I don't know how you met."

Malcolm got up from the table and walked to the window above the kitchen sink. He looked across his farmland and said, "We met at the Harvest Ball. The year was 1862, and I was home on furlough. I'd been a professor before the war." He looked over his shoulder at Abby. "In those days, the college was called Pennsylvania College. But I didn't teach history then. I taught mathematics." He turned back to the window. "When war broke out, I was immediately called up. My education at West Point included a specialty in cavalry. "

"And you still love being on a horse."

Malcolm returned to the table and sat down. "Yes, I do. Horses are intuitive, and I suppose they have filled a void for me. Relationships with people are far more complicated."

Abby leaned forward in her chair. "All those years you kept to yourself. Why did you choose me?"

He smiled. "You have a spark of determination that I find irresistible."

"You mean I'm stubborn?"

"More like unrelenting. You hold on and never let go to accomplish your goal. That is a quality I admire. If you insist on comparing yourself to Sarah, you are more than her equal in that regard. I've seen the way you've tackled this play, and I've watched you coach the student actors. You have fire in your belly, and that's a trait I've lost."

"Malcolm, you were the most inspiring professor I ever had, and your passion was contagious. If I'm a good teacher, it's because you set the bar so high."

Malcolm ran his hand through his hair. "After Sarah died, I didn't care about anything, but as I continued to walk this earth in my altered state, I wanted to honor her memory. We had both experienced the horrors of war, so when I started teaching history, my main objective was to make students see that war is never the answer. Robert E. Lee once said, 'It's a good thing war is so terrible; lest we enjoy it too much.' If mankind can't learn from history, we are doomed to repeat our mistakes. I was at a low point immediately after September 11, and that was precisely when you came to my office as a student. I had completely lost faith in mankind's ability to peacefully coexist."

"Leave it to me and my perfect timing." Abby rolled her eyes. "I thought I'd offended you, though I couldn't figure out how. You practically grimaced when I said you'd made a difference in my life."

"Actually, I cherished what you told me, but I wasn't ready to accept it. You'd seen something in me that I no longer saw in myself."

Abby touched Malcolm's cheek. "People give education a bad rap, but it's our first line of defense. There will always be wars, but you've given countless students a more accurate context for thinking about war. And I'll bet you've nurtured a pacifist or two." Abby smiled. "Like me."

"How did you become so wise?"

Abby leaned forward, elbows on table. "You inspired me." She chewed on her lip. "I feel honored that you've told me about your past, but I still don't know how you became a vampire."

Malcolm cupped her elbows in his hands. "I'll tell you—soon."

Chapter Sixteen

The play's premiere was fast approaching, and Malcolm needed time to think. Leaving the theater after rehearsal, he checked to make sure there were no spectators, and then launched into the night sky. He could have morphed to bat form, but it was less taxing to maintain human form while airborne. As he pierced clouds and glided toward the moon, he considered how much more free his life had become since he met Abby.

She'd enabled him to exercise his true nature through this play, and he had to admit the experience was therapeutic. Some days in rehearsal, he was so into his role he longed to dispense with living undercover. Even just a rapid move across the stage would provide the audience with some real shock value. It might be worth the sweet smell of their fear.

Oh, God, what was he thinking? He'd spent countless years taming his base desires and hiding his true self, but underneath his human exterior was still a vampire itching to display some fang. Would Abby ever understand that? Probably not, unless he made her a vampire. He picked up speed, soaring at the idea . . . to have her with him through eternity. But he would never coerce her. That would have to be her decision. He hadn't told her how he was turned, but he would soon. If she could accept that, perhaps she would join him.

Sarah had loved him as a farmer and soldier. He'd had no supernatural abilities to entrance her. He offered her everything he had, and that was enough for her. Since he became a vampire, he knew he could easily lure any woman, but he wouldn't use his hypnotic wiles on Abby. Though he'd kept his instincts in check, he had to wonder what attracted her . . . the flawed man or the vampire?

*

Abby gnawed on a fingernail, and then slapped her hand away from her face. The stage crew was a few days behind with the backdrops, and she wanted everything to be perfect. She'd arranged for the head of the theater department at NYU to attend the dress rehearsal in hopes of a scholarship or two for her students.

She paced the empty theater, arriving an hour ahead of the cast to double-check the sets. Yesterday, when the plywood moon fell from the boom light and almost conked the female lead, Malcolm had swept her out of the trajectory just before it plunged to the stage and broke into smithereens. Maybe she was being paranoid, but she had to wonder whether Pamela had loosened the moon. Although none of the cast had commented on the extraordinary speed of Malcolm's reaction, another malfunction like that might set them pondering about his super-human reflexes. Some days, he seemed dangerously vampiric.

Abby looked up at the tangle of wires and cables that crisscrossed the ceiling of the theater, out of sight of the spectators. A catwalk that suspended a string of stars swayed eerily above her head. Her students had done an amazing job on a shoestring budget. She hoped NYU would be impressed. The glittering stars, clapboard moon, and chiffon ghosts were effective, but with a real vampire as the star, Malcolm's presence overshadowed any props. She'd almost deep-sixed the dry ice the first time he glided across the stage. His uncanny grace didn't require a foggy backdrop, but then she decided that the fog might help disguise the glide.

She shivered, recalling the previous evening in his arms. He didn't often nick her neck in the heat of passion, but last night when his teeth graced her throat, he'd punctured her skin with his razor-sharp fang. He immediately sealed the wound with his velvet tongue and later apologized for getting carried away, but Abby had loved the surge of warmth the act sent to her core, spreading like elixir through her bloodstream.

The slam of the stage door jerked Abby out of her thoughts.

"I'm glad you're here." Kyle approached her, script in hand. "That scene where our vamp trails his tongue down the virgin's neck is not working for me."

"You must be joking," Abby said. "It's perfect."

"There's not enough tension. I'm not sensing her fear."

Abby shrugged. "She's enraptured, sucked in by his charms."

"Nah, it's too quick." Kyle rubbed his chin. "I don't think she should cave until he sinks his teeth into her neck. I'd like to see her be stiff, and then when he bites her, she can melt into him." Kyle reached for Abby's hand. "Here, let me show you." He tossed his script to the floor and stepped into Abby's space, entwining his fingers in her hair. She immediately stiffened. "Yeah, that's good. See how your shoulders screwed up under your ears?" With his other hand, he pressed his hand into her back and brought her close.

"Kyle, I don't think we should . . . "

His lips were at her ear, nibbling, and then the hand that had been at her back went south. She raised her hands to push against his chest.

"Am I interrupting something?" The echo of Malcolm's baritone bounced off the concrete walls.

Abby's heart kicked into overdrive. She sprang away from Kyle. *How much did Malcolm see?* Running her hands down her corduroy jeans, she said, "Kyle was just demonstrating how to build tension in the first bite scene."

"There's plenty of tension in that scene." Malcolm eyed Kyle with a look that could bore holes in wood.

Kyle's Adam's apple quivered. "I think the virgin should display more fear."

"She senses what's coming," Malcolm said. "She's apprehensive but not fearful. She wants to be bitten." Malcolm turned his gaze to Abby. His eyes glowed red. "All women do."

Abby took Malcolm's arm. "Malcolm, you need to calm down."

Kyle raised an eyebrow. "Is someone getting jealous?" He acted tough, but his voice trembled.

Abby's heart beat in her ears. Before Malcolm could answer Kyle's question, she blurted, "Don't push it, Kyle."

Kyle picked up his jacket and headed for the exit.

When Abby heard the door shut behind Kyle, she looked at Malcolm, whose eyes remained a glowing red. "He has no interest in me. If he did, he would have made a play long ago."

Malcolm balled his fists. "He was trying to rile me, and it worked."

"How is it you showed up just as the shark was circling?"

"I feel you, Abby. It's like radar. If you're in trouble, I'll know it."

"Wow, that's better than 9-1-1." She smiled. "But I wasn't really in trouble with Kyle."

"Perhaps not, but what he did was . . . disturbing."

"How could you possibly be jealous of Kyle?" She ran her fingers down his arm and captured his hand, which was icy cold. "Malcolm, your hand is freezing."

"I'm agitated."

He'd turned so white, he almost glowed.

Abby let go of his hand and pressed her fingers to his cheek. "Sometimes I worry I've pushed you too far, like I've cracked your cocoon."

Malcolm flexed his fingers. "I'll be all right."

"You say that, but you're tapping the floor to beat the band." She grabbed both his hands in hers. "What have I done to you?"

Chapter Seventeen

Over the theater's sound system, Abby listened to the clashing cymbals of Grieg's *In the Hall of the Mountain King*. The clanging built to a crescendo that would sync with the play's climax. She just hoped Malcolm's antics didn't overshadow the intense music. She was terrified he might reveal himself for what he truly was. In his role as the Gettysburg Vampire, he'd unleashed a side of himself that had been sequestered for one hundred and fifty years, and he seemed to be enjoying the experience a bit too much. Then there was the incident with Kyle, where a sudden streak of jealousy got the better of Malcolm, making his eyes flash crimson. With tomorrow's opening just a bite away, it was time for a heart-to-heart.

As usual after the evening rehearsal, he'd left the theater first. Then, she joined him at his house after she made sure the students had all left the theater.

She found Malcolm in the kitchen, making her a cup of hot cocoa, just one of a few new domestic duties he'd mastered since she entered his life. He'd also become adept at laundry. She spoke to his back. "As you know, I've done quite a bit of research on vampires. Are there other vampires who can function in daylight?"

Malcolm turned and handed Abby a mug. "A few, though aside from my maker, I don't know them. I inherited that ability—sort of a vampire genetic code. It's quite rare, and it's enabled me to mainstream."

"Tell me about your maker." The closer she got to Malcolm, the more curious she was about the process. If their relationship continued to develop, would she consider trading her humanity for immortality?

Malcolm nodded to the mug in Abby's hand. "I will—some other time. Drink your cocoa."

Abby wished he would be more forthcoming, but she decided not to press. She took a sip. "You're always making me something to drink, and you never drink anything."

"I can get down a good glass of cabernet, but it's not my favorite beverage." He waggled his eyebrows at her.

She shivered. "I don't dwell on your need for blood, but really, how often do you have to . . . imbibe?"

"Not often. When I was first turned, I was ravenous. All new vampires are. But over the years, as I've chosen to live a human existence, I can sustain myself on semi-monthly raids of the blood bank."

"The blood bank? Don't you feel guilty, taking blood that some hospital patient may need?" Abby screwed up her nose. "And how do you get in?"

"I only take tainted blood, Abby. It's not fit for human infusion, but it's fine for me. And I travel as vapor. I'm sure the personnel notice that there's product missing, but it's not useful blood, anyway."

Tamping down a wave of nausea, her hand instinctively went to her stomach. "I assume that sometime in your history you fed off humans?"

Malcolm's eyes grew dark. "Yes, I had to. But in spite of the many men I killed during the war, I've never killed anyone for blood. Besides, I wiped the memories of my donors, so they were none the wiser."

Abby frowned. "Does that mean you could wipe my memory?" The thought frightened her. Her life had inextricably changed in the last few weeks, and she couldn't imagine having what she'd experienced with Malcolm erased.

"No, my love, that only works for brief encounters. For better or worse, I am indelibly written in your history." He smoothed her eyebrow with his thumb, and then kissed her temple.

She sighed her relief, albeit unsettled. "Can we change the subject?"

"Absolutely," he said. "Tell me, what would you do if you weren't at the college? Broadway, perhaps?"

Abby rolled her eyes. "Heavens, no, I like being around the students. At some point, I'd like to do a workshop for underprivileged kids, like I did at NYU. Unfortunately, the current theater budget is extremely lean. The administration may decide they don't need two professors in the department, and Kyle has seniority. You, on the other hand, are irreplaceable at the college. You'll never lose your job."

"I suppose they'd be hard pressed to find another Civil War instructor who was also a veteran. Though I'm going to have to add a few gray streaks to my hair soon, or the faculty will think I've found the fountain of youth." He laughed.

Abby loved the sound of his laugh, a low rumble that started in his gut. She'd never heard him laugh before they became a couple. "How long have you been at the college?"

"This time around? Close to twelve years. I taught here from 1905 to 1915, and then I spent some time at the University of Virginia, earning my Ph.D. I returned to Gettysburg in the 1950s. I just have to make sure no one is still on campus to remember Professor McClellan when I reappear. And since I no longer show up in photographs—another vampire thing—there aren't any old yearbooks with my unchanging image in them."

"I wouldn't fret about your age giving you away as much as your attitude."

Malcolm's jovial expression morphed to an intense stare. "What do you mean?"

"I'm worried sick you're going to reveal yourself during this play." Abby set her mug on the kitchen counter and returned Malcolm's stare. "Those vampire goons could show up at any time, and one flash of a fang would be your death knell."

"Don't worry. I'll be able to sense them in the audience."

"Okay, so even if you don't do anything they could pick up on, the audience could freak out if you do something like move too fast."

"They'll think I'm a remarkable actor." Malcolm half smiled.

"Perhaps too remarkable." Abby rubbed her arms. Malcolm's house was always chilly. "Or what if Kyle sidles up to me, and you get jealous. Can you control that?"

He circled her waist with his hands. "Abby, Abby. I appreciate your concern, but I doubt any of our students, and I know none of the faculty, believe that vampires truly exist. They won't see what they aren't looking for."

"If they did suspect, could you wipe their memories?"

He laughed again. "No, that only works one-on-one, and I have to be looking into their eyes."

"I'm not reassured." Her hand went to her stomach. "I feel queasy about it."

"Be glad you can feel queasy. I don't remember most of the feelings I had as a human."

"But you remember love." Abby placed her hands on Malcolm's broad chest.

"Ah, yes. That I remember." He wrapped his arms around her.

Abby snuggled into his embrace. "I don't need to have children, Malcolm. I'm dedicated to teaching, and some of the best teachers I've had over the years have been childless."

He pulled back and looked at her. "That's a big decision, Abby. What brought that on?"

"I just wanted you to know what I've been thinking about."

Chapter Eighteen

As the premiere of the play approached, the vampire goons were making regular appearances at rehearsals. Their glowing red eyes distracted and disturbed Abby.

Later that evening, back at Malcolm's house, she paced the living room. "You have to do something about those guys. If you don't, I will."

Malcolm settled in his wing chair. He grabbed Abby's hand as she brushed by. "Ignore them, Abby. That's what I'm trying to do."

"Are you crazy?" Abby glared pointedly at him. "They could destroy you. One false move on that stage, and they'll be flying to the council. Is that what you want?"

Malcolm ran a hand through his hair. "Abby, have you given serious thought to where your life is heading?"

"Did you just change the subject?"

"No, not at all. Have you thought long term—about us?"

"Constantly. You are my life, Malcolm. I don't want to live without you, and if anything happened to you, I . . . " She looked away before he could see her tears.

Malcolm turned her chin back to face him. "I've already been responsible for one woman's death."

"You weren't responsible for Sarah's death. The war was." *I wish he could let go of his guilt.*

"If I hadn't been part of that war, she wouldn't have been involved."

Get tough, Abby. "For a smart man, that's an idiotic thing to say. You were a West Point-trained cavalry officer. You *had* to be in the war."

"True, but I didn't have to be *incommunicado.*"

"And disobey orders? That doesn't sound like the Malcolm I know." She pointed her finger at his chest. "You can't live your life on 'what ifs,' and you can't change the past."

"There you go, acting wiser than your years, again." Malcolm ran his knuckles across Abby's cheek.

She caressed his hand at her cheek. "Please, back to the subject at hand. Promise me you won't do anything to provoke those guys."

"You mean by being me?"

"I mean by being too *much* you. I have enough to worry about with Pamela after my job. I don't need to worry about some vampire council passing judgment on you."

"I'll try not to get lost in the moment. I think you call that method acting, right?"

"Precisely, but in this case it's a dangerous technique. It could get you killed."

"I'll be fine. And I'll take care of Pamela. Just because I don't use my wiles on you doesn't mean I can't make her see the error of her ways."

"She's nastier than she looks, so watch out."

Malcolm reared his head back and laughed. "My dear, I'm a vampire. We wrote the book on nasty."

*

Malcolm spotted Pamela crossing the quad ahead of him. He caught up with her and grabbed her elbow. "I believe you have something of mine."

"Geez, you scared me." She squinted through light snowflakes at Malcolm. "I didn't hear anyone behind me."

"Maybe you should pay better attention to your surroundings." He smiled for a micro-second. "Young women have been known to disappear from this campus." Even he could hear the menace in his voice.

"Thanks for the advice, Professor. I didn't know you cared." Her smile was much longer than a micro-second and delivered with lowered eyelashes.

"You haven't answered my question, Miss Shields." He hadn't let go of her elbow and now he squeezed it.

"Ouch." She tried to brush off his hand, but his grasp was firm. "I didn't hear a question."

"It was more of a statement. You have something of mine."

She blinked. "I do?"

"Yes. The gown you took from Miss Potter's office belongs to me. It's a family heirloom."

"I have no clue what you're talking about."

He widened his eyes and zapped her with a shock of vampire glamour.

She froze, her face expressionless. "Come . . . and . . . get . . . it."

"Excellent. When?"

"Tonight . . . my apartment . . . 380 Lincoln Drive . . . eight o'clock." She licked her lips.

Malcolm let go of her elbow. "See you tonight." As he strode away, he looked back over his shoulder to find her glued to the same spot, staring after him. He smiled. She'd shake it off in a minute, though she'd still crave him. Would she greet him tonight in a negligee? The thought wasn't appealing. He might have glamoured her more than he'd intended.

*

Abby shook her head at Malcolm's account of his meeting with Pamela. "Oh, to be a fly on the wall. Could I come with you tonight?"

"She may be glamoured, but she's not stupid. She'd snap out of it if she saw you."

Abby removed her gloves and warmed her hands at Malcolm's fireplace. Staring into the flickering flames, she shuddered.

He wrapped his arms around her from behind. "Cold?"

"No. I was just thinking about how easily you entranced her. You could do that to me."

He turned her around and held her shoulders. "I wouldn't."

"But you could." She took a step back, bumping the fireplace screen. "It makes me feel like I don't have free will . . . that you could coerce me."

He sighed. "Abby, you never have to worry about that."

She rubbed her arms. "I want to believe you."

He turned from her, walking to a window where the bleak winter landscape reflected the abrupt change in his mood. "This is why I've avoided a relationship for so many years. I wasn't sure I could keep myself from behaving like a vampire. It's our nature to want to bring people under our spell. It's essential to our survival. If we didn't glamour humans, and then wipe their memories, we couldn't feed off them."

"You know how creepy that sounds?"

"Of course, I do." He looked back at her, and there was pain in his eyes. "When I rescued you from the Goth club, I could have easily glamoured you into sex. But I wanted more from you, Abby. I wanted you to care for me as a man."

"I do care for you. I . . . I . . . " How could she put into words the depth of her feelings for him?

"Hear me out. I know you admire my humanity, but you also have to accept that I am not human. And you have to believe me when I say that I will not coerce you . . . ever." He ran a hand through his hair. "Damn, Abby, I thought we'd been over this."

"We had. It's just that when you told me how easily Pamela succumbed to your glamour, it scared me."

"Does this scare you?" He opened his mouth, and his fangs extended. Involuntarily, Abby jumped. She wished she hadn't.

Malcolm closed his mouth and squeezed his eyes shut. When he opened them, his half squint showed his sorrow. He swiped a hand across his face, and then checked his watch. "I need to go and be a vampire for a while. Will you be here when I return?"

"I'm not sure. I, I . . . need some time to think." He'd grazed her neck with his fangs before, so why in heaven's name did the sight of his fangs frighten her? Hadn't she accepted his nature?

Malcolm's tires screeched on the gravel as he left for Pamela's apartment. Abby almost ran after him, but she didn't know what to say. Yes, she was extremely attracted to him. He was more than attractive. He was magnetic, sexy, and forbidden. That aspect of him, his vampirism, was both exciting and frightening. There was a whole side of him that she couldn't fathom and a million reasons why she should run the other way. She could second-guess and analyze, but in the end, it was just her and her heart. Like Pat said, don't intellectualize feelings.

He'd demonstrated over and over how much he cared. He'd rescued her from the Goth club. He'd put himself in danger by acting in her play, and now he was solving her problem with Pamela. He'd risked everything for her, and what had she done? Acted like he had a contagious disease. And why? Because she thought he might glamour her. Didn't she trust him? No one had ever made her feel the depth of passion and longing that Malcolm did. With him, the heat inside her became something all its own. And once again, he was out there being courageous for her while she was sitting on her keister.

What could she do for him? She thought about those creepy vampires who had been hanging around the theater, hoping he'd trip up. Malcolm's way of dealing was to ignore them, but Abby watched them as they took notes on his performance. They were gathering evidence that he was displaying vampire characteristics. One flash of fang, and the vampire council would descend on him like a cannon ball in free fall.

She checked the clock on the mantel—eight-fifteen. If she left for Philly now, she could be back by midnight. She'd formulate a plan on the way. Surely, they'd listen to reason.

*

Malcolm pulled up to the curb in front of Pamela's apartment and turned off the ignition. He squeezed the steering wheel of the truck he'd bought to haul his horse trailer. His life had been uncomplicated when all he'd had to think about was his curriculum and where the next Civil War re-enactment would take him. But it had been empty, too. Devoid of feeling.

Now he had feeling . . . in spades . . . and where had it gotten him? The woman he loved was repulsed and frightened. It was little comfort that she cared about Malcolm, the man, because his human side was only part of his being. Since he'd agreed to this play, opportunities to exhibit his true nature had erupted at every turn. If he wasn't on stage, acting the part, he was glamouring a woman. He'd suppressed that ability for more than a hundred years.

Until the twentieth century, he'd glamoured his share of people. Whether women or men, he'd needed to feed. A brief lick over the puncture wound provided instant healing for his victim, and a moment of eye contact wiped the memory of his deed. It was a cold, cruel existence, but at least his victims walked away unscathed and unaware. Not the best rationalization, but he was after all, a vampire.

He assuaged his guilt over Sarah by his dedication to teaching, to making a difference in the world. And in her memory, he vowed to lead a human existence. With that vow came the pledge to imbibe only bottled blood, which had tempered his animal desires . . . until he allowed Abby to invade his heart. But he wouldn't trade a minute of the time he'd spent with her. For better or worse, she'd crept into the farthest reaches of his heart, places where the pumping and flushing of blood didn't reach. Places where nothing could dislodge the love.

Malcolm didn't know how long he sat in the car, staring at a tear in his dashboard. When he looked up, Pamela was on her stoop, blowing frosty breaths and glaring at him. With a heavy sigh, he opened the door and swung his legs down to the icy pavement.

He grinned as he approached. "It's cold. Go back inside."

"I've been watching you from the window," she said. "You've been sitting in that car like a statue. I came outside to make sure you hadn't died behind the wheel."

"I assure you, I am . . . here." *Dead, but here.* He'd been correct in anticipating her attire. She was shivering in a black, knee-length robe with a plunging neckline and feathers at the hem.

"Come in." She opened the door with a flourish and led Malcolm inside. "I bought a few sex toys specifically for this occasion. Shall we give them a try?"

Malcolm was incapable of being shocked, but her comment made him take a step back. He *had* come on too strong with the glamour. "I'm not here for pleasantries, Miss Shields."

"Please, call me Pamela." She rubbed against him like a cat in heat.

"Just give me the gown."

"That old thing? You're welcome to it. It gives me the heebie jeebies."

"Why did you take it?"

"I thought it might have some value, since Abby coveted it. But I can't even take it out of the box. It shocks the heck out of me." She licked her lips. "Tell you what, you can have your silly gown, but only if you do the nasty with me first." She batted her eyelashes so fast they vibrated.

Malcolm was completely out of practice with the glamour. With one glance, he'd turned a well-bred woman, albeit bitch, into a horny streetwalker. He scanned her living room, hoping to locate the box that contained Sarah's gown.

Pamela clucked her tongue. "I see what you're doing, looking around for that gown. You think you can grab it and get out of here, but I wasn't born yesterday. I've got it well hidden."

Seems he'd gone far enough with the glamour to make her libido rage, but not far enough to bend her will. "Let's sit down and talk, Pamela." He motioned to her black leather sofa.

"I'm all for a little pillow talk, but let's do it in my bedroom." She took Malcolm's hand, but when she tried to pull him toward her bedroom, he wouldn't budge.

"No, we'll do it here." He pushed her to the sofa.

She pouted, but then sat on the sofa and patted the space next to her.

Malcolm sat and turned to her. He took her chin in his hand.

She fluttered her eyes shut and pursed her lips . . . like a guppy.

"Cute." Malcolm shook her chin and forced her to look at him. "Pamela, I'm going to tell you how things are going to be. I'm in love with Abby Potter, and I will not bed another woman. You are not half the woman she is, but you have a chance to redeem yourself. Here's what you're going to do. You're going to bring me the gown, and then you're going to pack your bags and leave Gettysburg. Never come back here. When I walk out your door, you will not remember what happened this evening. You will only know that you have an overwhelming desire to leave." He let go of her chin. "Now, be a good girl."

Pamela blinked a few times, and then looked down at her negligee . . . and gasped. She scurried to her bedroom, returning in record time with the box Malcolm had requested. "I think this is yours. I don't know why I had it." She shrugged, and then crossed her arms over her breasts. "Sorry for my inappropriate attire. I was just practicing some lines from *Cat on a Hot Tin Roof,* and I wanted to feel the part."

"You'll make a great Maggie," Malcolm said as he walked out the door. He turned to give her one last stare . . . for good measure. "Goodbye."

He placed the box on the passenger seat of his truck. Opening the lid, he carefully separated the tissue and breathed a deep sigh when the gown appeared to be unharmed. "Thank God," Malcolm said out loud. He gently touched the fabric.

His heart sped as he drove to his farmhouse. Would Abby be there?

When his truck hit the gravel of his driveway, he stopped abruptly. Abby's car was gone. His immediate inclination was to drive to her apartment, but then he sensed her fear. Like the day he'd returned home those many years ago and knew something horrible had happened to Sarah. Abby was in danger.

He pounded the steering wheel with his open palms. He closed his eyes and willed his mind to conjure her location. He got snippets of a neon sign, the smell of bourbon and smoke. And then he knew.

Spinning out of the driveway, he gunned the accelerator and headed to Interstate 95. If he drove like a bat out of hell, he could make it to Night Fright in half an hour. He considered resorting to bat form, but no other mode of transportation would get him there quicker than his truck. If the police nabbed him, he'd glamour them.

He peeled off 95 and was in Night Fright's parking lot just moments later. It seemed exceptionally quiet. For a weeknight, Malcolm supposed that wasn't too unusual. Abby's car was one of only five cars in the lot.

He strode to the bar and slapped his hand on the varnished wood to get the bartender's attention. It was the same walleyed, vampire bartender who'd been there that first night when Malcolm rescued Abby.

"Uh, what can I get you?" The bartender swept the room with his good eye.

"You know damn well why I'm here. Where's Abby Potter?"

"Don't worry. We won't hurt her as long as she cooperates."

"Where is she?" Malcolm grabbed the bartender's collar and pulled him halfway across the bar.

A door behind the bar swung open, but when the vampire who was exiting saw Malcolm, he quickly retreated.

Malcolm followed. The door led to a short corridor. He heard whimpering from a lighted room at the end. His heart leaped. If she was hurt in any way, he wouldn't contain his rage. He burst into the room.

Abby was sitting in a chair behind a desk, seemingly unharmed. She had a pen in her hand, and a vampire behind her had his hand wrapped around hers, trying to make her sign something. Two other vampires flanked her.

"I'm who you want," Malcolm said. "Let her go."

"Malcolm, no!" Abby looked up at him, fear in her eyes. Whatever they wanted her to sign, they hadn't glamoured her to make her cooperate, which struck Malcolm as odd. But these were young vampires. Perhaps they didn't understand the nuances of glamour and only used it to feed.

The vampire who held Abby's hand smiled broadly, revealing yellow fangs that matched his bleached hair. "You've been careless, Professor. All we need her to do is sign this affidavit, confirming what she knows. The council will take it from there."

"I won't sign anything," Abby said. She looked at each of her captors.

Malcolm calculated his chances of killing the three vamps in the room and rescuing Abby. Even if he could get her out, he'd have to kill the bartender, too, and any other vamp he encountered on the way out. He couldn't leave any evidence. Because of his age, he was stronger than these vampires, but his skills at fang-to-fang combat hadn't been tested for more than a century. Still, he'd do whatever it took.

The bleached blond grinned and bent his head to Abby's throat.

Malcolm backhanded him across the face. "Don't touch her."

The vampire snarled, and then a lascivious grin curled the corners of his pale lips. "Or you'll do . . . what?"

"I shouldn't have to tell you that my blood is ten times richer than yours, which makes me ten times stronger," Malcolm said. "That thin stuff streaming through your arteries is like Boone's Farm to my Bordeaux. I could take you all out in a matter of seconds." More like half a minute, but intimidation couldn't hurt.

"Now, hold on, Professor." This from the vampire who'd opened the door. "We all value our immortality." He smirked. "We're not here to off anybody, but since the little lady knows your secret, we can't let that go unnoticed by the council. Humans are forbidden to know about our world."

"Wait a minute, fellows," Abby said. "I've gone along with this charade because I always enjoy good role play, but what 'secret' are you talking about?"

The vampires stole quick glances at each other.

"Don't play dumb," Mr. Bleach said. "You know damn well that the professor is a vampire."

Abby let out a hoot. "Right, and I'm Marie Antoinette. Look, I can appreciate you like to have a little fun, and I'll admit that the professor makes a great vampire, but he's *acting*. I hate to burst your black bubble, but I don't believe in vampires. I know you guys think you're the real thing, and I'm not one to pass judgment on your idea of a good time. It's a free country, but if you don't mind, I'll get my jollies elsewhere."

Malcolm could do nothing but stare at her, nor could the other vampires in the room.

"What do you think of thith?" The third vampire displayed his fangs . . . with a lisp.

Abby rolled her eyes, and then yawned. "Look, this has been fun, but I've got classes tomorrow, and I need to get home." She rose from the chair and stretched. "Thanks for the entertaining evening." She looked around her. "I must have left my purse at the bar. I'll just get it on the way out." She pointed to the door, and then walked out of the room.

Malcolm made eye contact with each of the vampires before turning to leave.

"Just remember, Professor." Mr. Bleach tapped him on the shoulder. "We'll still be watching you."

*

Abby didn't slow her forward momentum. She swung her purse from the barstool to her shoulder, walked out Night Fright's main entrance, and then broke into a trot to her car. She had no doubt Malcolm could handle himself with those goons, and when she heard someone else come out of Night Fright, she stole a glance over her shoulder. Malcolm motioned for her to get in the car.

Once she was on 95, her cell phone chirped, displaying Malcolm's name. "Was that a close call or did we have some wiggle room?"

Malcolm chuckled. "Hard to say. Those guys can't assemble a critical thought between them, so I half expected one of them to either lunge at me or sink their fangs into you."

Abby shuddered. "I'm just glad I didn't have to swear on my mother's grave that I don't believe in vampires. She wouldn't have appreciated my taking her name in vain."

"Not to mention that she isn't dead."

"True." Abby sighed. "Thank God."

"You were brilliant—and brave."

"A girl does what she has to do, and I wasn't up for witnessing a blood bath. You would have killed those guys."

"I'd do anything to keep you safe, Abby. You are everything to me."

"I know." Her voice shook.

"You created your own cyclone back there. You see now what I mean when I call you 'proactive?'"

"I suppose. The thought just popped into my head that I could fool them. Now that it's over, it seems surreal. "

"Promise me you won't take a chance like that again. You were brave, but it wasn't the smartest move."

"I know. I didn't think it through before I hopped in my car. I thought I could reason with them."

"They don't reason. Sure you're okay?"

"I think it's finally sinking in."

"Do you want to pull over and let me drive? I can pick the other car up later."

"No. I'm all right. I just want to go back to your house. And get naked."

"You're starting to sound like a vampire. Near-death experiences are an aphrodisiac."

"Must be the company I keep. Oh, wait, I don't believe in vampires, remember?"

Chapter Nineteen

Opening Night - December 16

Abby blew on her cold fingers and shuffled her feet, which wasn't easy in three-inch heels. She watched Kyle's mouth move but was too nervous to pay attention to his words. If he hadn't looked her way and nodded, she would have completely missed her cue to take the stage.

She allowed herself one cleansing breath, and then counted the steps slowly that led to the microphone.

"Good evening, faculty, students, and Gettysburg residents, and thank you, Kyle, for that lovely introduction." *Whatever you said.*

"The holiday play is a tradition at the college, and I am pleased to have participated in its success for the past three years. This year, however, I have an added responsibility as the playwright, so I'm more nervous than usual. I hope that any failings in my prose will be more than compensated by the delightful performances of our stars, Karen Thompson, a junior theater major, and Dr. Malcolm McClellan, professor of Civil War history. They are joined by a fine supporting cast. I trust you will find *Vampire Train* to be a wild romp through an era of love and war, of parasols and cannon balls. And for your protection, the stage crew will be passing baskets of garlic cloves. If you don't need them to ward off a vampire, you can save them for your pasta *puttanesca*. Now, please join me as the curtain rises on Act One."

Abby swept her hand across the stage and backed away from the curtain as the heavy velvet drapes crept upward and strains of eerie music from the sound system pulsated toward the full house. Once concealed in the left wing, she had a straight-on view of stage right, where the actors were set to enter. She shifted her feet and counted to ten. Malcolm materialized out of thin air and met her gaze across the stage. When she smiled at him, he winked back, and then glided onto the set. His larger-than-life presence—ironic for a dead man—captured the stage. The music stopped and Malcolm spoke.

"Good evening." His deep baritone echoed in the silent theater. "I roam the streets of this city at night, searching for what I loved and what I left unfinished."

Uh-oh, that wasn't in the script.

Abby swiped a finger across her forehead, catching beads of perspiration in spite of the theater's lack of heat. She listened closely as the Gettysburg Vampire introduced himself to the audience and regaled them with Civil War history and his conversion to immortality. He was improvising, and with intensity that hadn't been present in rehearsals. Goose bumps rose on her flesh, and she waved her arms at Malcolm, hoping to get his attention. She knew his vision could take in a more expansive landscape than any human, so she wasn't surprised when he looked her way.

Careful not to step within the view of the audience, she made a chopping motion across her throat. Malcolm raised one eyebrow at her and returned to his soliloquy.

"There are days when I hardly remember what it was like to be human," he said, pacing the full breadth of the stage, "and then there are days when I almost think I *am* human."

Karen wandered onto the stage, swinging a parasol. *Good grief, she's only supposed to use that in the daylight scenes.* Maybe she was just so nervous she had to have something in her hand.

As the Gettysburg Vampire saw her, he said, "The evening is becoming more interesting." He glided toward her from behind, tapping her on the shoulder. When she turned and gasped, he caught her at the waist and peered intensely into her eyes. "It isn't prudent for a young woman to be out at night," he said, "but you are safe now."

Abby held her breath. Something was going on with Karen. Though she was playing a part in which her character was required to fall under the vampire's spell, in all the rehearsals she'd seemed to be acting. Abby watched Karen's eyes glaze over as she swooned, and then fainted. Yes—fainted—dead away. And she wasn't acting.

At this point, the vampire was supposed to sweep the maiden into his arms and exit stage left, cueing the stagehands to lower the curtain and begin set-up of the next scene, which took place at the vampire's home. However, Abby didn't wait for Malcolm to carry Karen off the stage. She signaled for the curtain to be lowered as soon as Malcolm caught the unconscious Karen. She had about seven minutes to talk with Malcolm before the next act, and she needed to make a few points abundantly clear.

The curtain had barely brushed the floor when she stormed onto the stage and grabbed Malcolm by his rock-hard bicep. He was fanning the face of his "victim." Abby motioned offstage for some smelling salts, and then she said to Malcolm, "I need a word—now!" She pointed to stage left.

Kyle came running with a capsule of ammonia as the stage crew scurried to bring in living room furniture and a fake staircase. Karen flung Kyle's hand away from her face as the broken capsule stunned her to attention, and Kyle helped her to her feet.

"Let her rest for a few minutes," Abby said to Kyle. "We can delay Act Two if she needs more time." Abby retrieved a tissue from her pocket and mopped Karen's brow. "Just a touch of stage fright, Karen. Don't worry. It happens to all of us. Take some deep breaths." She patted Karen's hand. "Have a few sips of water." Abby nodded to Kyle, and with his arm around Karen, he helped her off the stage, though the smirk on his face told Abby that he was pleased as punch with this calamity.

Abby turned to stage left, where Malcolm waited for her in the shadows. She tromped toward him and steered him behind a rack of costumes. His eyes glowed red. "No wonder you scared the hell out of her." She punched him in the chest to no visual effect. "What are you doing out there?"

"I'm being myself." His neon eyes were the only things Abby

could see as they huddled in the dark corner.

"That's just it. Don't be yourself!" She clamped a hand over her mouth, worried she was being too loud, and then she contemplated the rafters. When she looked back at Malcolm, she said, "I can't take this, Malcolm. I've been a nervous wreck for the past few weeks, worried sick you'd expose yourself. I haven't seen those vampire goons in the audience tonight. They may have bolted when we handed out the garlic, but that doesn't mean they won't show up." Abby huffed and folded her arms across her chest.

The redness of Malcolm's eyes faded, and he spoke in hushed tones. "Just don't wave one of those garlic bulbs in front of me." He smiled. "I will admit that I'm enjoying the opportunity to play a role that is my nature, but I'm not going to bite my leading lady—much as I might be tempted."

"I can't believe you said that." Abby took a step back, bumping into the costume rack.

"This has nothing to do with my feelings for you. It's the animal in me. I've controlled my base nature for more than a century, but a pulsing vein is difficult to resist."

Abby stomped her foot. "What's become of my life?" She threw up her hands. "Damn you, Malcolm McClellan. Damn you for making me fall in love with you." Abby swiped at the welling tears in her eyes, and then shoved the costume rack out of her way. She turned from Malcolm and without looking back at him, said, "For your own sake—*behave.*"

As she began to walk away, the vise of Malcolm's grip on her arm stopped her.

"Who do you love, Abby? Malcolm the man . . . or the vampire?" he asked hoarsely.

She whirled around to face him. "I think you're the most incredible, smart, sexy man who's ever walked this earth. I'll admit aspects of your nature have scared me, but they don't overshadow the remarkable man you are . . . inside." Abby clenched a fist and punched the air. "Oh, God, I can't talk about this now. Just remember, this stage may be the only place where you can be yourself, but you have to do it in a way that doesn't ruin your life . . . as a professor."

Malcolm squinted at her. "Perhaps you really do love me."

"Oh, for Pete's sake, you *would* finally realize that at a time like this." Abby rolled her eyes, though it was just as much *her* realization. She did love this man.

"You don't have to worry about me revealing myself, Abby."

"It's more than that. I also feel that this play has made you recall the life you had with your wife, and frankly — " she drew a deep breath and then exhaled "—I'm sorry I've forced you to relive those painful memories."

"I'm not sorry, Abby. I'm grateful. I'd locked my heart away, and I didn't feel worthy of love." He reached for her, but she jerked away from his touch. "This play has made me remember many things in my life I'd suppressed. I haven't wanted to recall what happened during the war and the fateful role I played, but you've brought me closure. By putting my 'what ifs' behind me, I can finally look forward to a future. I have a new perspective . . . and a reason to live."

Tears streamed down her face, but she held her palms up in front of him. "I don't know whether to hug you or slap you. Your new perspective couldn't have come a moment too soon. Now, go out there and be you." She shook her head. "No, don't be you. Be a reasonable semblance of you. And please—" She thumped her fist to her heart. "Please . . . be careful."

"Rest assured. I am a vampire, but I don't have to act it out on a stage. The woman I love believes in me, and that is everything."

Chapter Twenty

Abby's first exhalation came about ten minutes into Act Two. Reminding herself to breathe, she clenched and unclenched her fists. She'd stood on the sidelines with every sense tuned to the subtleties of Malcolm's performance. Though she'd adjusted to and even appreciated the traits that made him more than human—like the immediacy of his reactions and the intensity of his stare—nothing he did in the second act seemed more than good acting. Even Karen recovered enough from her first act swoon to deliver a convincing role as the vampire's love interest, parasol and all.

The cast beamed as a standing ovation from the audience signaled an encore bow, and Abby breathed a deep sigh of relief. But her elation was short-lived.

Kyle had been noticeably absent from the cast party. Just a few students remained as Abby and Malcolm left the theater.

At one a.m., the dark campus turned eerily quiet. Only the hoot of an owl disturbed the solitude. Abby shivered in the frosty night air.

*

"Attendez, professeur." The voice whispered across the night sky.

Malcolm froze. He'd recognize that voice anywhere, and it wasn't simply the French language. The breathy inflection could only belong to one person, Michel Auchamp, the chancellor of the vampire council. Malcolm pulled Abby behind him to shield her. "What do you want, Auchamp?"

"No formal greeting, Malcolm, after all these decades?" Auchamp dropped his French.

"I respect your age, Auchamp, but I don't agree with the direction of the council. You know that." Malcolm felt Abby's breath catch at his words. No doubt she'd opt for a more diplomatic approach.

"I must admit we thought you would betray yourself through this play, but since you offered no *corpus delicti*, we have had to act outside our edicts' jurisdiction. We did not count on you exhibiting such restraint, but I suppose that is what comes from your many years of humanity."

Malcolm heard rumblings of many voices on the wind. Had Auchamp brought the entire council with him for this confrontation?

"Again, Auchamp, what do you want?"

Auchamp's laughter shook the branches of an ancient oak and rattled an owl from its perch. The owl circled Malcolm and Abby, and then returned to the tree.

"My dear Malcolm, all we want is your cooperation."

A chill ran up Malcolm's spine. As he straightened, Abby's arms tightened around him. "The word is coercion, not cooperation."

Auchamp laughed again. This time, the owl hooted, fluffed its feathers, and resettled. "Call it what you will. We haven't harassed you because we thought we could find your trait elsewhere, but after an exhaustive search, we haven't been able to locate a single vampire immune to the sun. And since you've been reluctant to create any vampires with your unique quality, you're our only hope. A few pints of your blood should enable us to create a strain of creatures with your special attribute."

"Why is this so important? Vampires have been creatures of the night for thousands of years," Malcolm said.

"We cannot make our mark on the world without entering politics, and to do that, we need to come out of the darkness. Soon, we should have enough vampires working in the daylight to make an impact on the world. We will be able to infiltrate every aspect of society once we are not restricted to nightfall. And since your girlfriend's boss has been such an able accomplice, we're going to let him be our first recipient."

On cue, Kyle stepped from behind the oak, flanked by his Night Fright brethren. "And a delighted guinea pig I am."

"You bastard!" Abby shrieked. She stepped from behind Malcolm and pointed a finger at Kyle. "If you think I'd let you use Malcolm's ability for evil, you don't know me very well."

"Oh, I know you, Abby, and your honorable boyfriend, too." Kyle chuckled. "But power isn't based on honor, and these guys have the power." Kyle swept his arm across the sky, and suddenly, dark shapes took form and drifted to earth, landing without a sound.

Malcolm quickly counted eight imposing vampires, each of them as old as him, which meant they would all be as strong as he was. This was far from the situation he'd faced with the Night Fright boys. He could take the council members one-on-one, but two or three of them could easily pin him down. They'd have no trouble strapping him to a board and getting his blood. "I'll leave with you willingly, but Abby walks."

"Nothing doing," Abby said. "You've lived a noble life, Malcolm. You've used your gift to help generations of students become better people. You can't let them have your blood."

"Abby, we have no choice." Malcolm tugged Abby back to his side and wrapped his arm around her shoulder. She had no idea what they were up against. If he lashed out at the council, they'd subdue him and make him watch them drain Abby. As it was, the more agitated she became, the more fiercely her heart beat, and a thrumming human heart at this close proximity could only be tolerated for so long. If he didn't get her out of here soon, they'd descend on her. And when they were through, there'd be nothing left but her boots.

The council formed a semi-circle around Malcolm and Abby, and they slowly encroached.

Abby gasped as Michel Auchamp ran his tongue over a fang and sneered. "She smells positively delectable, Malcolm. We may need to rethink our purpose here this evening."

Malcolm tightened his grip around Abby's shoulder. His mind raced with options for escape. None. "You came for me. Let her go."

Michel moved one step closer to Malcolm and Abby. He inhaled deeply. "Her fear is seeping out her pores. I do not believe I can resist." He bent to Abby, his eyes ablaze.

Malcolm grabbed Michel by the throat, but before he could give a good squeeze, the other council members pounced, pinning him to the ground. He couldn't move a muscle. "Just take me now. Drain me. You can get human blood anywhere. You don't need her. I'm the one you came for." He watched the slow dance of seduction build in Michel's eyes. The old vampire had set his course.

"Don't look at him, Abby," Malcolm said just before a fist punched his jaw, and then clamped over his mouth.

But it was too late. Abby had fallen under Michel's spell. She gazed up at him as he ran his finger down her cheek. He rested his index finger on the pulsing artery in her neck, and like a lab technician would tap the spot to bring it closer to the surface, Michel did the same to Abby's carotid.

Malcolm writhed to free himself, but at least ten hands subdued him. They increased the pressure and held him still. He bit the hand on his mouth, and then a blow to his temple disoriented him. When he was able to refocus, Michel's tongue tickled the spot on Abby's neck where he would puncture her porcelain skin. Even his worst nightmares couldn't compare to the terror of this moment.

Abby's eyes closed as she leaned into Michel's embrace. He cradled her head in one hand and bent her back. His other hand crushed her pelvis to him, and Malcolm watched as Michel rubbed himself lasciviously against her. He summoned every ounce of his strength to break his captors' hold, but chains couldn't have held him more tightly.

Michel turned to Malcolm. "I am wondering how she will taste. Tell me, Malcolm, will I be able to stop drinking her? I feel I owe it to my compatriots to allow them at least a few ounces of this precious elixir." He smiled. "But sorry fellows, this little coquette is all mine. In fact, what was I thinking? I cannot simply drink her. I shall multi-task." The hand that had been grinding Abby's body into his moved to the front of her jeans and began a slow rub.

Until he'd met Abby, Malcolm had frequently considered how sweet death would be, and now he wanted nothing more than to live . . . with her. From the depths of his being, he assembled a strength borne of love. Against all odds, he churned with a will that transcended logic and physics, and he broke free.

*

Startled by swift movement in her peripheral vision, Abby's head snapped to Malcolm. Though disoriented from the glamour, her body jerked as she looked back to Michel's face. She immediately closed her eyes, and then she eased a hand into the little purse she wore across her body. She'd stuck an extra garlic bulb there from the handout at the play, just in case she ran into one of the Night Fright boys. Crushing the bulb in her hand, she smashed it into Michel's face.

Michel screamed.

Strong arms wrapped around her waist and pulled her away from Michel.

Temporarily distracted by the distress of their leader, the vampire council rushed to Michel's side as Malcolm backed away with Abby in his arms.

*

And then feathers flew.

The owl launched from its branch and scraped its talons across Michel's head, causing the old vampire to pull back and scream. Blood from the gouges the owl inflicted oozed out of his scalp and down his forehead.

The owl landed at Michel's feet, and then began spinning. Malcolm thought the creature would burrow into the ground from its whirling action, but amidst flying feathers, it rose and grew. As the spinning slowed, feathers morphed to brightly colored cloth. The jingle of hundreds of bells accompanied the show. A mane of curly hair settled on a purple crocheted shawl.

Pat, the costume mistress, smoothed down her skirt and patted her mane. She cleared her throat. "I apologize for my late arrival. Sorry I was unable to intervene earlier, but I only expected the Night Fright boys to be here. I hadn't anticipated the whole shebang."

Malcolm had long known Pat was a witch, and though she was dedicated to the forces of good, he'd always given her a wide berth, and not just because of her size. In spite of super strength and immortality, vampires were helpless under a witch's spell.

"Who are you, old woman?" Michel blinked at Pat through his blood-soaked eyes.

"Old woman, eh?" Without further preamble, Pat swung her arm over the vampire council and the Night Fright boys, Kyle included. As though she were speaking in tongues, a voice emanated from her that wasn't her own. Deep and melodious, her Latin chant vibrated on the wind. Malcolm caught a few of the phrases, like "*a mari usque ad mare*," which he took to mean that whatever she was intoning would last from sea to sea.

The vampires stood mesmerized through her chant, and when she finished, with a deep bow, they looked at each other like they had no idea why they were there.

"Malcolm McClellan, what a lovely performance. We wanted to commend you." Michel tipped Malcolm a salute, and then looked quizzically at his bloody fingers. "Uh, we will leave now." He nodded to the members of the council, and in unison, they sprang up and disappeared in the dark sky. The Night Fright boys followed suit. Only Kyle remained.

"Yeah, good performance," Kyle said, shaking his head. He sauntered off in the direction of the theater, and then changed direction in favor of the faculty parking lot.

Once Kyle was out of sight, Abby turned to Pat. "What in the world did you do to those guys?"

Pat shrugged. "I just wiped their knowledge of why they were after Malcolm. That's why they all looked so clueless. And don't worry about Kyle. I fiddled with his state of mind. Any day now, he'll tender his resignation from the university. He's heading for Montana."

"Montana?" Abby asked.

"Big bad Kyle wants to be a cowboy."

"I'd hate to see him at liberty, even with cows." Abby winced.

"When the time is right, I'll conjure a fitting demise." She tapped her nose. "A stampede could be fun, with Kyle in the middle."

Malcolm pulled Abby close, and then gagged.

"Oh, sorry. I forgot about the garlic." She held her hand out, away from his face.

Malcolm recovered enough to speak, "How can we ever thank you, Pat?"

"Shucks, I live for this stuff." She brought Abby in for a hug, shook Malcolm's hand, and sashayed off, jingling all the way.

*

When they finally reached the solace of Malcolm's house, Abby hurried inside to wash the garlic off her hand. Returning to the living room, she removed her coat, throwing it over the back of Malcolm's wing chair. She took a few deep breaths. "For the first time in a very long time, we don't have to watch our backs."

"I was ready to take to the sky with you in my arms, and then Pat intervened."

"You saved me." Abby touched Malcolm's cheek.

"We saved each other, my love. That garlic provided the perfect distraction."

"Yeah, but you'd have gotten us out of there."

"We could have made our escape, but we'd be forever watching our backs. We'd have to move far away from Gettysburg." Malcolm walked to the fireplace, picked up a poker and stabbed at the spent logs. He placed two new logs on the grate, lighted a folded newspaper and stoked a new fire.

"Well, Pat solved that." Abby chuckled.

Malcolm turned from the fireplace. "If Pat hadn't wiped their memories, would you have left all you know and escaped with me?"

"Of course, Malcolm." Abby walked to him and wrapped her arms around his waist.

He cradled her head in his hands. "It's time you heard the story of how I became the creature I am."

"So, you're finally going to tell me. Is this because you want to make me a vampire?" The prospect of joining Malcolm's world . . . for eternity . . . gave her heart a jolt.

"Only if it's what you want."

"I've been so worried about you revealing yourself through the play, I haven't thought much about me in the equation."

"Equation?" Malcolm stared into Abby's eyes.

Abby could tell from his blank expression that he had no idea what she was talking about. "Yes, you know—one human female plus one vampire male equals . . . ?"

"Ah, that equation." Malcolm nodded. "You are clearly the essential factor."

"I'm not sure how you figure that. You'll live until the end of time, and I've got about twenty years at best before my wrinkles would make you look like a gigolo."

Malcolm grinned. "I'd relish being your gigolo."

"This isn't funny, Malcolm." Abby disengaged from his embrace, backed into the wing chair and sat, her arms folded across her chest.

"I'm sorry, love. No, it isn't funny, and I apologize." He sat on the footstool in front of Abby's chair. "Over these past weeks, I've seen how much you care for me, and I have fallen deeply in love with you. I think I've known it since I rescued you from that bar in Philadelphia. I took one look at those spiderweb earrings, and

I was hooked." He reached behind her head, gathered her hair up and held it in a temporary ponytail, then let it go. "I could spend eternity just twirling your hair between my fingers."

Abby's heart did a somersault, but she didn't buy his timing. "You weren't in love with me at that bar. You may have been attracted, but you were also annoyed."

"I wasn't ready to hear the truth. I knew I'd become a rote imitation of the teacher I used to be, but you nailed me. I also needed to be sure you weren't like any number of women who are captivated by vampires. I knew you were different, but I didn't completely trust you. But you've showed me your true character, Abby. I'm in love with you, and I think you really love me."

This was the man she wanted to spend the rest of her life with, but if she remained human, his life wouldn't track with hers. What if she became a vampire? A jolt of electricity shot up her spine. Yes, it made perfect sense. "I do love you, Malcolm."

"And now there is something I need to tell you—something I've never told anyone." Taking both of her hands in his, Malcolm began his story.

Chapter Twenty-One

I lay on the tracks, motionless. The humid and still air hung like a veil around me, with the only sound an occasional robin's call. The rails would provide no vibration from the ghost train, and no whistle or smoke would herald its approach.

With my men stationed behind the trees, I was alone and vulnerable. If the train stopped and the ghosts proved menacing, I'd be defenseless.

A chilling breeze crept over my skin and briefly stirred the hair on my arms and chest. I tensed. Through the merest slit between closed lids, I glimpsed the outline of the locomotive's enormous wheels, gleaming silver against the sunlight. The breeze intensified as hands of bone rather than human flesh grasped my legs and shoulders, lifting me. The touch was icy but gentle, and no sounds of exertion accompanied their task, though I weighed two hundred pounds.

I didn't dare open my eyes to see where I was being transported, but when I was placed on a pallet, I sneaked a look. Five gray uniforms. I braced myself. It was time to let my captors know I wasn't dead. To steel my courage, I allowed myself a brief thought of Sarah—the taste of her lips as she'd kissed me goodbye. I took a deep breath and emitted a low groan.

"He's alive, captain," one soldier said. "Get the general."

As though regaining consciousness, I slid my eyelids open and blinked several times to clear my vision. I tried to rise up on one elbow, but collapsed back on what I could now see was a cot. "Where am I?" I looked around the room, counting four soldiers. They looked solid, not like the spirits I'd seen in battle, though their skin was as gray as their uniforms.

"You're on the Stonewall Jackson," said a soldier whose shoulder bars indicated he was a captain. "Who are you?"

I began to speak but was interrupted by the arrival of a man I'd seen only in photographs—a man who had died of pneumonia after having his arm amputated from a wound he'd received at Chancellorsville. I'd been there, across the battlefield from the second most revered general in the Confederacy. Now I looked into the sharp eyes of Stonewall Jackson.

"What were you doing on the tracks?" General Jackson asked, his tone threatening.

I ground my teeth before replying. The general seemed to be looking into my soul. No room to dissemble. "Trying to repair them, sir. My men and I have been following a small group of rogue Yanks who've moved into Northern Virginia."

The general stroked his thick beard and looked around at his group of soldiers. "I suppose you realize by now that our train doesn't depend on tracks."

I thought hard about how to answer. "I'm privileged to be in your presence, general. I've heard tales of the ghost train, but I had no idea you were on board."

General Jackson nodded. He looked me up and down. "What happened to your clothes?"

"Well, sir, it was so hot working on the tracks, I figured we should just do it in our skivvies . . . sir." I gave a humble half smile. I was in skivvies because my only alternative was my Union uniform, and that would have been an immediate giveaway.

The general nodded, again. "Welcome aboard, though I'll be damned if I know what to do with you." His eyes seemed kind, but behind their friendliness glinted a hint of red. I figured they were bloodshot, and then I registered something stranger. The general's color was not gray like the other soldiers. He looked pale, yet alive. "Where are you injured, soldier?"

"I must have been hit on the head, general. We were repairing the tracks when we were ambushed by some fellows on horseback. I remember seeing someone swing at my head with a rifle butt." I touched the back of my head gingerly, and then winced. "Frankly, I don't know why he didn't just shoot me. Don't know where my men are, whether they got away or were captured. I guess the Yanks figured they killed me."

"Do you have a knot on your head?" General Jackson moved closer to me, and I detected the faint scent of lemons on the general's clothes. I remembered hearing that Stonewall was particularly fond of the fruit.

I turned my head so the general could see the wound. "I believe the knot's gone down, general."

The general reached out and touched the back of my head, and then he brought his fingers to his nose. A sinister smile curved his lips. "Interesting scent. How was the meat?"

My heart beat faster in my chest. "Pardon me?" I'd used rabbit's blood on my fake wound.

Stonewall Jackson addressed the ghost soldiers who were now hovering over his shoulder. "Leave me, men. I need to speak with this man—alone." He turned away from me and monitored the departure of his men. When he rounded on me, his fangs protruded over his bottom lip. "I know the difference between human blood and rabbit blood, soldier."

My skin prickled. I watched Stonewall's eyes drift to my neck, and I instinctively brought my hand to my pulsing vein. A rush of cold fear skittered down my spine. "You're not gray like the ghosts. What are you?"

"I am what people call 'undead.'" The general snickered. "Now tell me—truthfully—why are you on this train?"

I found myself leaning toward Stonewall, whose eyes captured mine in a mesmerizing stare. Before I could conjure a believable lie, I blurted the truth. "I have direct orders from General Meade to investigate the train."

The general shook his head and harrumphed. "I'm only surprised it's taken the Yanks this long to send a posse. And who are you?"

"I'm just a soldier who wants this war to be over so I can return to my wife and farm, general."

"Like any soldier, no matter which side he's on. And what are you fighting for?"

"I am opposed to slavery, general, but I understand how Southerners feel about states' rights. If I were a Virginian like you, I'd probably want to be left alone to govern on my own terms."

The general's expression softened and his fangs sank back into his mouth. "I have a wife and baby daughter at home in Lexington, but I can never return to them." He shook his head. "Still, soldier, you haven't told me your name."

"I'm Colonel Malcolm McClellan of Pennsylvania, general."

"Well, Colonel McClellan, you've been bold to board this train, and I can use a bold man."

I held Stonewall Jackson's stare as the general stroked his long beard, no doubt contemplating my fate. "I feel I can trust you, Colonel McClellan, and I'm rarely wrong about anyone." Stonewall half smiled. "Since I became a vampire, I'm an even better judge of human character." He paced the railway car.

"I'm not afraid of you, general," I said. "I believe you to be an honorable man."

"I am, and that didn't change when I became a vampire. I won't harm you, but you're going to need to do something for me."

"Before you ask, I would never betray my men, general."

Stonewall shook his head. "No officer worth his salt would do that. But you must promise me that you will no longer fight against the Southern cause. That's no more than I'd require of any prisoner of war."

"Yes, general, I've demanded the same of captured Confederates. I will abide by those terms." I raised my hand in a salute, and Stonewall returned my gesture. We had sealed our agreement in a way that we both knew was binding.

"I'm going to let you go home to your wife, but first you must visit my wife and daughter in Lexington." Stonewall looked out the window at the passing countryside. "You can tell her you were a soldier in my corps, and you wanted to return the sash she made me." Stonewall smiled. "I know you can act. I've seen you play a convincing role in your skivvies. But this time, you'll be in a Confederate uniform. That should help your ruse."

*

I visited Mary Jackson and her infant daughter, Julia, in Lexington. I held Mary's hand while she cried over her husband, and then I bounced baby Julia on my knee. She was a beautiful little thing, and holding her made me miss Sarah all the more, imagining her heavy . . . someday . . . with my child.

"How well did you know my Thomas?" Mary asked.

"I suspect I knew him as well as a soldier can know his superior officer," I said. I wondered if my regiment would say the same of me.

"Thomas was a fierce soldier, but he was also a very tender-hearted man." Mary wiped a tear from her eye. "He loved children, and he was devastated when our first daughter died. I am so sorry he didn't live to be part of Julia's life."

I took a handkerchief from my pocket and handed it to Mary. "I'm sure your husband is here in spirit, and he lives in Julia." I tilted the baby's chin. "She has her father's brow."

Mary swiped her eyes with the handkerchief, and then smiled. "Yes, she's her father's daughter."

When I said goodbye to Mary and Julia, I asked if I could do anything for them.

"You've already done so much, colonel," Mary said. "You've been a real comfort to Julia and me. If you have an opportunity to return, I would welcome your visit."

"I don't know where the war will lead me next, ma'am, but I would be honored to visit you, again." I kissed Julia's forehead and handed her back to her mother.

"Where are you headed now, colonel?"

I rose from the settee and settled my hat back on my head. "I'm heading home to see my wife for a few days, and then I'll report back to my regiment." I touched Julia's foot, covered in a crocheted bootie, and thought of the tiny socks Sarah had been making in hope of a child. "You take care of this beautiful baby."

"Keep your head low out there, colonel, and thank you." Mary followed me to the front door. I felt her eyes on my back as I walked to my horse. Mounting the steed General Jackson had provided, I tightened the reins, and then touched the brim of my hat in a parting salute to Mary and Julia.

It took seven days to reach my farm—seven days of hard riding on back trails, keeping to the woods. I wore the Confederate uniform into Maryland, and then changed to a faded chambray shirt and dungarees that Mary Jackson had given me. In exchange for the yellow sash I'd returned to her, she'd packed a few of Stonewall's civilian clothes that she thought I could use when I returned home.

I didn't know where my men were—my loyal men. I hoped they were all right. Had they remained in Virginia, waiting for my return, or had they doubled back to Pennsylvania with the news that I'd been abducted by the ghost train? Sarah didn't need to hear that.

My pulse quickened. I was almost home. But as I crested the ridge, the house seemed eerily still. What day was it? Would Sarah be at market? I spurred the horse to a gallop, and then reined him abruptly as our hired man, Sully, came running from the barn.

"Colonel," Sully shouted, "thank God you're home."

"Where's Mrs. McClellan?" I asked as I dismounted, tense with foreboding.

"Oh, colonel, something terrible happened. Mrs. McClellan had been nursing the soldiers in town, and there was an outbreak of typhoid fever. She came down with it, and she's awful sick. She's in town at her sister's house."

My heart stopped, and then a roaring sounded in my ears. I'd intended to water my horse, but instead, I remounted and steered the stallion toward town. The only thing that mattered was getting to Sarah as quickly as possible.

I skirted town and took back streets to avoid running into anyone I knew, racing against mounting storm clouds and distant lightning. When I reached Caroline's, I jumped off the horse and slung the reins around the hitching post. I burst into the house and yelled for my sister-in-law.

Caroline appeared at the second story landing. She staggered when she saw me. Gripping the staircase with one hand, she motioned for me to come up the stairs. She grasped my shoulders as I reached the top step. "Malcolm, where have you been? Didn't you get my letters? I was frantic to find you. Why didn't I hear from you?" She pounded my chest and then fell against me.

I wrapped my arms around her. "I'm sorry, Caroline. I haven't received letters for weeks." If only I'd known, I'd have rushed to Sarah's side. Damn the war and this foolhardy mission.

"She got deathly sick about ten days ago, and then she rallied. I thought she was out of the woods, but then the fever came back. Oh, Malcolm, if only you'd been here."

"Where is she?" My eyes darted around the landing.

"She's in my room. I wanted her to have a nice window to watch the birds. But she's delirious today. She wakes up for a few minutes and asks for you, and then she collapses. I'm frightened, Malcolm."

I hastened to Caroline's bedroom and rushed to Sarah's side. She was flushed with fever, her breathing ragged. I picked up her limp hand and brought it to my lips.

"Last time she woke up, she was pinching the air for angels' wings." Caroline put a hand on my shoulder.

"What does that mean?" I brushed tendrils of Sarah's hair away from her face.

"It means the angels are near, and she's reaching for them." Caroline's voice caught on a sob.

"Bring me a basin of cool water," I said, "and a clean cloth." My eyes didn't leave Sarah's face, and I gently stroked her temple. "I'm here, my darling. You're going to be fine. I'll be strong for both of us. I'm not going back to my regiment. The war is over for us, Sarah. Just please, please stay with me." My eyes filled with tears, and I blinked hard to clear my vision. I took her hand. "If you can hear me, squeeze my hand."

Sarah's eyelids fluttered. She opened her mouth to speak, but the only sound was a deep sigh. She smiled weakly.

Caroline returned with the basin of water and a cloth. I dampened the cloth and applied it to Sarah's hot forehead. "There now, don't try to talk. I love you with all my heart."

Sarah took a slow breath, and then her chest seemed to sink into the feather mattress. She did not inhale again.

"Sarah!" I pulled her limp body into my arms. "Sarah!" I rocked her and buried my face in her hair. "No! No!" Caroline's trembling hand pressed my shoulder as I continued to sway on the bed and sob. "Please wake up, my darling. Don't leave me."

"She's with the angels, Malcolm. Let her go." Caroline knelt by the bed and clasped her hands in prayer, her tears pooling on the quilt. "She suffers no more."

"No, she's just sleeping. She can't be gone. She can't be." I picked Sarah up and carried her to the window. I turned her head to the view. "There's your favorite oak, Sarah, with the cardinal's nest, remember?"

"Put her back in bed, Malcolm." Caroline patted the mattress. "I'll send for Reverend O'Donnell." She pushed herself up slowly.

"No, we don't need the reverend. Sarah just needs to rest. She'll be fine in the morning. Won't you, love?" I kissed Sarah's forehead, and then placed her back on the mattress. I watched as Caroline folded Sarah's hands across her chest. "There now, rest," I said. "I'll check back in a little while. We have so much ahead of us, Sarah."

I staggered out of the room and collapsed in the hall.

For the next three days, I couldn't eat and could barely speak. Caroline had the doctor administer laudanum to get me through the nights.

We buried Sarah with her Bible.

At the funeral, the mourners assumed I had been granted leave. My men had not returned to Gettysburg, so no one knew about the ghost train. Many townspeople offered condolences, but all I could do was nod. My heart was a dark cavern from which I felt I would never emerge.

But out of my despair, a plan coalesced. When I left Caroline's, telling her I had to go back to my regiment; I knew what I would do. I owed it to Stonewall to return to the train and report on Mary. I only hoped the general would honor my request.

Chapter Twenty-Two

"So, you asked Stonewall Jackson to make you a vampire?" Abby wiped tears from her eyes. The poignancy of Malcolm's story gnawed at the pit of her stomach.

"Actually, I asked him to kill me, but he wouldn't do it. I told him I couldn't do it myself. I wanted to die a soldier's death, an honorable death at the hand of the enemy. And then he came up with an alternative. He'd never turned anyone, but he'd be willing to make me a vampire. Speaking from his own experience, he told me that emotional pain is not as intense for a creature of the night. Though he missed his wife and daughter, being a vampire gave him a different perspective. I didn't understand how it could be any different, but if he wasn't willing to kill me, I told him I'd take the next best thing."

"Becoming a vampire, you mean?"

"Yes, though the irony is that I missed Sarah just as much after I was turned, and becoming a vampire did nothing to assuage my guilt. What Stonewall hadn't accounted for was the fact that his wife and daughter were still alive. Even though he missed them terribly, he had hope for their future, whereas my wife was lost to the ages." Malcolm got up from the footstool and walked to the mantel. He stared into the fire.

Abby left the wing chair and wrapped her arms around his waist, pressing her face to his back. "If you'll let me, I'll do everything in my power to make sure you never feel that kind of pain again."

Malcolm folded his arms around hers. "You've already brought me out of the darkness, Abby."

With her head still pressed against his back, Abby asked, "Why didn't General Jackson visit his wife and daughter himself?"

"He thought it would be too much of a shock for his wife. She'd seen him ensconced in a coffin, laid in the ground, and covered with dirt."

"Okay, I need more information here."

Malcolm turned to face Abby. "Sorry. Let me explain." Malcolm ran a hand through his hair. "Stonewall didn't die from his arm amputation. He was recovering from the surgery when he contracted pneumonia, and that was the fatal blow. The doctor who attended Stonewall knew the day he was going to die, and told him so. But he gave Stonewall a choice. He offered him the alternative of immortality."

"So, the doctor was a vampire?"

"Yes. He actually turned Stonewall on the day everyone else thought he died. New vampires need a couple of days of complete rest before they can emerge in their altered state. The doctor bit Stonewall, and ordinarily in vampire creation, the inductee would then bite the vampire. But Stonewall was in such a weakened state that the doctor bit himself on the wrist and let the blood trickle into Stonewall's mouth. The doctor called Stonewall's family back in the room and pronounced the general dead. Two days after the funeral, the doctor returned to the gravesite and uncovered Stonewall Jackson, vampire."

"Fascinating. Is that the key to becoming a vampire, drinking vampire blood?" Abby's heart raced, but not with fear.

"Yes, you would be bitten so the vampire could first mingle your blood with his, and then you would bite the vampire and take a small quantity of co-mingled blood. If you think of it like a blood transfusion, you can only be infused with your blood type. Any other blood type would kill you. By co-mingling the vampire's blood with yours, you can tolerate the transfusion."

Malcolm's face lacked expression, and Abby knew it was for her benefit. This was her decision. A few weeks ago, the prospect of exchanging blood would have made her gag. Today it was fascinating . . . and sexy. She'd struggled, trying to separate the man from the vampire, but now she saw that the Malcolm she loved was both . . . and better for it. His dedication to Sarah had translated to his teaching, and now he offered that same dedication to her. She was ready for his world.

"All right, Miss Curious. Surely there's more you want to know?"

Abby pursed her lips. "You mean about becoming a vampire?"

"Yes."

"I've made up my mind about that, professor, but let's finish your story first. What happened to Stonewall's wife and daughter?"

"I continued to visit them after I was turned. They never knew I was a vampire. Mary became a champion for perpetuating the general's memory, and Julia grew into a lovely young woman. Unfortunately, she died in childbirth when she was in her twenties."

"How about your family—and Sarah's?"

"Caroline was already a childless widow, and she died a few years following Sarah. The rest of my family was scattered around Pennsylvania. They assumed I'd gone missing like so many of the soldiers in the war, and I thought it best to let them believe that. About forty years after the war ended, I returned to Gettysburg with the deed to my house. I passed myself off as Colonel McClellan's grandson. Squatters had set up residence, and it was a mess. It took me more than a year to refurbish the property and the grounds. And as I've told you before, I've had to leave a few times because of my agelessness. If I stay away long enough, no one is left to remember me."

Abby nodded. "And that's always worked for you?"

Malcolm chuckled. "I had a close call once. The eighty-five-year-old widow of the mayor insisted I was a dead ringer for a professor she'd known at the college. I was more than a dead ringer, but I was able to persuade her that everyone has an identical twin in the world."

"What about the ghost train? Did it simply disappear? And where is Stonewall?"

"When the war ended in 1865, there were no more casualties to collect, at least not in a wholesale way. Soul catchers mobilize around war and natural disasters, and then they disperse when they're no longer needed. The train was abandoned by the ghosts, and the locomotive is now in a museum in Virginia. There's a plaque that says it was such a powerful steam engine that rumors suggested it flew. As for Stonewall, he couldn't bear to be in this country following the war. He moved to England. I continued to correspond with him until the 1940s. Last I heard he was a pilot in the Royal Air Force." Malcolm smiled. "Any more questions?"

Abby touched the lapel of Malcolm's tweed jacket and fingered the buttonhole. "No questions, but I do have a request. You're shared your soul with me, Malcolm, and now I'm ready to share mine with you." She eased four fingers into the band of his wool slacks.

Malcolm cocked an eyebrow at Abby but didn't say a word.

"I believe we were destined to be together. When I look back at the choices I've made, they all led to us. Returning to Gettysburg after graduate school was about *us*, and writing the play was about *us*. Even all the time I spent trying to avoid you was about *us*. I've struggled with reconciling who I am with the amazing woman who was your wife, but I finally realized that no matter who Sarah was, she could not have loved you any more than I do. Nothing is more important to me than being with you. This is my home, wherever you are—forever. I want to be a vampire."

"You can't know how lonely my life was until you sauntered into my office in your paint-spattered jeans. You've left a handprint on my heart, and I feel whole again." Tucking a tendril of her hair behind her ears, Malcolm leaned in and whispered, "I thought I'd never love anyone the way I loved Sarah, but I was wrong. If you knew how much you mean to me . . . "

Abby shivered as Malcolm traced her ear with his tongue. "Does it hurt, becoming a vampire?"

"There may be waves of nausea and lightheadedness but

nothing unbearable," he whispered huskily, "and I'll distract you."

Abby pulled back and looked directly into Malcolm's eyes. She saw love and joy there. "I'm ready."

"Are you absolutely sure?"

"Surer than I've ever been of anything. There are so many ways I want to show my love for you. I can't do it in a lifetime. I'm going to need eternity."

He took her hand. "Before we go upstairs, you have to promise me something."

"Anything."

"You have to marry me."

Abby smiled. "Well, that's easy."

"Come with me, love." He backed toward the stairs, pulling her with him, and then he swept her into his arms.

She kicked off her shoes, feeling weightless in his strong arms. When they reached his bedroom, the red tinge of his eyes glowed as he set her gently on the bed.

He smiled. "I'm going to kiss every inch of you."

Abby closed her eyes to feel his fingers lightly trace a sensuous journey down her body. She raised her arms and on this cue, Malcolm slipped his hands under the billowy silk fabric of her blouse, coaxing it over her head.

She had never been more aware of the blood coursing through her veins, blood that would soon be her beloved's. She reached up to his hair, and entwining her fingers in his ebony locks, brought his mouth to her neck.

About the Author

Susan Blexrud divides her time between Orlando, Florida, and the mountains of North Carolina. She is married with two adult children. Formerly the director of communications for the city of Orlando, she currently spends her days as a community volunteer, quilter, bird watcher, Yoga and Zumba enthusiast, and conjuror of her next romantic tale.

In the mood for more Crimson Romance? Check out *Witch's Soulmate* by Denyse Cohen at *CrimsonRomance.com*.

In the legend for plate Editor-in-chief, Printing of Chicago, we also
published in Revised Color, and we would want you.